THE SURGEON'S ONE NIGHT TO FOREVER

ANN McINTOSH

MILLS & BOON

First published in Great Britain 2018
by Mills & Boon, an imprint of HarperCollins*Publishers*
1 London Bridge Street, London, SE1 9GF

Large Print edition 2019

© 2018 Ann McIntosh

ISBN: 978-0-263-07835-0

MIX
Paper from
responsible sources
FSC™ C007454

This book is produced from independently certified
FSC™ paper to ensure responsible forest management. For
more information visit www.harpercollins.co.uk/green.

Printed and bound in Great Britain
by CPI Group (UK) Ltd, Croydon, CR0 4YY

To Michael.
Your love and belief give me wings.

CHAPTER ONE

A FRESH START. That was how Dr. Cort Smith thought of his position at Hepplewhite General.

A new beginning, far away from Denver, the snide remarks and pitying glances he'd gotten after being dumped by his fiancée just weeks before the wedding.

It was the type of move he now wished had been possible right after his honorable discharge from the army five years previously, but it hadn't been. He'd had a promise to fulfill, and now, having done so, was free to go on with his life.

The New York City job couldn't have come at a better time.

When he'd applied for the trauma surgeon position at Hepplewhite General, the board members who'd interviewed him had explained the hospital was undergoing a period of expansion and regeneration. There had been a sizable, anonymous donation, which, coming at exactly the right time, had allowed them to purchase land where an old warehouse had stood and begin construction to increase their capacity by twenty percent.

As the surrounding neighborhood was also undergoing some regentrification, they'd been able to raise additional funds to revamp the emergency room and surgical floor. Hepplewhite had always been rated a level two trauma center but the plan was for it to be ungraded to a level one, once all the improvements were finished. Cort didn't mind that things were in flux. Serving in the Army Medical Corps had made him pretty much immune to chaos and, since he'd wanted to move from Denver as soon as possible, taking the job had been a no-brainer.

Walking alongside Chief of Surgery Dr. Gregory Hammond, Cort tried to take in everything the older man said, although he knew, from experience, it was only with time that he'd remember it all.

"There have been, in the past, some…friction between the ER staff and the surgeons, but we're working assiduously to iron everything out before the expansion of the hospital is complete. Once we're upgraded to a level one trauma center, we must have things running smoothly."

"Of course."

No doubt he'd find out soon enough what types of friction Dr. Hammond referred to. Yet, in Cort's experience, there were always disputes between ER and Trauma, no matter how smoothly the hospital was run. That was just a product of human nature, and the instinctive need most doctors had to be in control.

They'd toured the surgical floor, and Cort was aware of the stares and murmurs of the staff as Dr. Hammond and he passed by, the searching glances of those he was introduced to. Not unusual, or unexpected, since everyone would want to check out the new surgeon, but he'd started to feel a bit like a specimen in a bottle. Something strange, like a teratoma, or a two-headed fetal pig—seldom seen and therefore gawk-worthy.

It didn't really bother him, though. He'd gone through too much in his life to be annoyed or made uncomfortable by others' curiosity.

Downstairs now, Dr. Hammond was showing him the construction zone, explaining what the various rooms still being built would be and how the new configuration would work.

"The expansion should be completed in about four to six months, and we'll be hiring new staff to fill the newly created positions in Trauma. There will be a slowdown in our emergency intake, so all the departments can be set up, and, as the board of directors indicated, you'll be assigned some general surgery cases to keep you busy."

Dr. Hammond turned down another corridor lined with heavy plastic sheets to contain the dust, beyond which a construction crew was working. There was a flurry of sound as an air hammer started up, and then the cacophony was overlaid by shouts.

"Hey, stop—stop—stop—*stop*!" followed by a string of curses so foul they would have made a sailor blush.

Dr. Hammond's face took on the pained expression of a man not used to such salty language, and he picked up the pace, heading for the exit at the end of the corridor. Once on the other side of the door, the noise reduced to almost nothing, he jerked a thumb over his shoulder.

"Sorry about that. Huh, construction workers."

His disgusted tone made Cort's hackles rise, but he didn't have time to say anything as just then the other man's cell phone rang. Taking it out, Dr. Hammond glanced at the screen and was already moving away as he said, "Excuse me a moment, Smith. It's my assistant."

Cort sighed. His annoyance faded, to be replaced by amusement at the memory of the older man's expression, but with it came familiar pain.

Brody had cursed like that all the time, even when he hadn't been on a job site.

"My goodness, Brody. Not in front of the kids," his wife, Jenna, would say after a particularly colorful outburst.

Hearing it had sometimes felt like going back in time to the foster home where Cort and Brody had met as teenagers. Except back then the admonition would usually come with a backhand slap from one of their foster parents too. Brody and Cort had always agreed that the place wasn't the worst either of them had been in, but they had both been glad to age out of the system and leave it behind.

They'd stayed close, even when life had taken them in different directions, Cort to the army and Brody into construction. The only reason Cort had returned to Denver when he'd been on leave, rather than travel the world the way he'd always wanted to, had been to see Brody and

Jenna. He'd stood as godfather for their son, had luckily been on leave and in the hospital waiting room when their daughter had been born. They'd been the closest thing to family he had.

Brody's death had sent him reeling and, coming just before Cort had been due to reenlist, had seemed like a sign. How could he not have known his best friend had been in so much pain? He'd known, of course, about Brody's original, job-related injury, but not that his best friend had descended into a full-blown opiate addiction. Jenna said she hadn't known either, but that didn't make it any easier to deal with. Cort felt as though he *should* have known, despite being so far away.

He'd always promised Brody to look after Jenna and the kids should anything happen, but leaving the army hadn't been easy since it had been his life for so long. But there really hadn't been an option, and he'd headed back to Denver when his tour was over and his contract had expired.

Now, in hindsight, he realized he'd been drifting along ever since.

Even getting engaged to Mimi had been done almost unthinkingly. She was Jenna's cousin, and she and Cort had gotten close during the dark days following Brody's death. It had felt good to be a part of Jenna's wider family, and when Mimi had hinted it was time to get married, Cort had agreed without thinking too deeply about what that entailed.

Three weeks before the wedding she'd called it off, saying she just didn't think it would work out. That she'd realized she didn't love him enough to be his wife, and she'd already found someone else.

After months of soul-searching, Cort knew he'd been unfair to Mimi. In a way, she'd been a crutch, holding him up after Brody's death. An imperfect replacement for the companionship he'd lost.

Despite the embarrassment and hurt, he'd known she'd been right not to go through with it.

Brody had always been the one who'd longed for a family, for roots, while Cort had wanted to see as much of the world as possible. Perhaps the difference stemmed from the fact Brody had lived with his mother until the age of seven, and knew what it was like to be a part of a real family. Cort had never had that, and knew he wasn't cut out to be a part of a family, didn't even know how to be.

Apparently he wasn't even fit to be a family member by proxy either since, soon after, Jenna too had cut him loose.

"Me and the kids, we'll be fine," she said, while they sat on her back step. "Mimi is a flake for waiting so long to break things off, and I know you're just hanging around here because of us. Brody always said you wanted to see the world. Go. Do it."

The sadness had weighed so heavily in his chest he'd been unable to even look at her. How many evenings like this had he and Brody sat in this same spot, beers in hand, talking? The twilight sky had gleamed between the branches, and a cool wind, harbinger of fall, had rustled the leaves, making them whisper and sigh. Her words had felt like another rejection, in no way softened by the squeeze of her fingers on his shoulder.

It was then he'd accepted that nothing good in life lasted. He was better off not getting attached, because to do so just brought heartache.

But this was a new day, full of potential and future adventure, and he wasn't going to let the past encroach on it. Shrugging off his dark thoughts, Cort wandered along the corridor, away from the chief surgeon and the construction zone.

At the end of the corridor was a T-junction, with a bustling nurses' station on his right and, as first one person and then the next turned to look at him, he once more became the cynosure of all eyes. Making eye contact with a few people, he nodded and smiled, until a noise to his left caught his attention, and he turned to look.

A woman stood at an exit door, holding a travel cup and tucking a cell phone under her chin. Something about her carriage, her profile made Cort's heart stumble over itself. And, as she turned slightly to swipe her access card to open the door, for the second time in less than five minutes his world tilted on its axis.

It can't be.

Yet, as she used her hip to push open the door and slip outside, he knew he wasn't imagining things.

It definitely was the woman he'd met in Mexico, who'd given him the most sublime night of pleasure he'd ever had, and had then run out on him without a word.

Without even giving him her name.

Worse, he'd confided in her about being dumped just before his wedding. No doubt, with the way hospital grapevines worked, that tidbit of news would be on everyone's lips by the following day.

A sour sensation filled his stomach, and all the anticipation regarding his new job leached away in an instant. It didn't matter that he didn't plan on staying at Hepplewhite very long. He'd only signed a one-year contract and, although the board had made it clear they hoped he'd renew at the end of that time, the plan was to move on to somewhere else. Have another adventure.

Right now, though, this felt less like an adventure and more like a mistake.

So much for a fresh start.

Cell phone held to her ear with one shoulder, Dr. Liz Prudhomme stepped out into the quiet of the staff parking lot and let the door swing shut behind her. Although there had been a midwinter thaw of sorts along the east coast, it was still cold, but after the dry heat of the hospital the damp chill felt good against her face. Grabbing the phone before it slipped, she found an alcove out of the wind and took a sip of her rapidly cooling coffee.

She normally didn't make personal calls while on duty, but her mother had just flown in from Milan the day before and this was the first opportunity Liz had had to speak to her. With the time difference between New York and California, it was perfect. Her mother would have just finished breakfast.

"The dress is delightful. Giovanna picked a strapless mermaid gown, made completely of Guipure lace. It's elegant and suits her so well. Although the designer isn't one I would have chosen, I have to admit it is beautiful."

In Liz's opinion, her future sister-in-law could wear a gunny sack and still look gorgeous. After all, Giovanna modeled for some of the world's best designers and probably wore a size negative three. Pulling off a dress like the one her mother was describing wouldn't be difficult for her at all.

Even if she wanted to, that wouldn't be the case for Liz. When it came to height and bone structure, she'd inherited her father's mostly Anglo-Saxon genes, rather than her mother's mix of Latin and Asian. She had a farm-girl sturdiness that once upon a time had been the bane of her existence. Now she was proud of her strength, and confident in her womanhood.

Most of the time.

Unless she let old insecurities rise up and blindside her.

But it wasn't jealousy making Liz feel out of sorts as she listened to her mother breathlessly give her all the details of the dress and their subsequent orgy of shopping. It was the usual feeling of inadequacy, knowing her ex-beauty-queen mother would have loved to have a daughter like Giovanna, rather than the one she had. Someone as passionate about fashion and decorating as Lorelei Prudhomme was herself. A daughter who could follow in her footsteps and excel at being a member of high society, not single-mindedly focused on her medical career.

Better to be useful than decorative.

Funny how often, at times like these, Nanny Hardy's voice popped into her head, reminding her of what was important. The nanny had left when Liz was eight, but her legacy was lasting.

"I don't know why they chose New York for the wedding." Lorelei sighed the special sigh that usually turned all members of her family to mush, and had them falling over themselves to give her whatever she wanted. She'd learned, however, that it didn't work on the strong-willed Giovanna. "It would have been so much nicer here in San Francisco."

Liz stifled a prickle of annoyance at hearing the same complaint for the hundredth time but just replied, "It's where Giovanna and Robbie wanted to have it."

"I know." There was no missing the pique in her mother's delicate tones. "But it's so inconvenient for us, really."

So said the woman who flew to Milan to look at a wedding dress, and help her future daughter-in-law shop for a trousseau! Liz shook her head silently, amusement making the corners of her lips quirk. Her anxiety, which always made itself known whenever she spoke to her mother, abated slightly. Taking another sip of her coffee, she swallowed her instinctive, somewhat snarky reply along with the strong brew.

"However, I'm sure it will be lovely. Giovanna has exquisite taste. Are you bringing anyone to the wedding?"

Caught off guard by the quick change of subject, although that was her mother's usual style of conversation, Liz said the first thing that came to mind. "Highly unlikely."

As her mother sighed again, Liz got that familiar sense of being not quite enough of a woman to suit.

Despite it being eight years since Liz had had a serious romantic relationship, her mother never stopped hoping, asking leading questions whenever the opportunity arose. Although she'd never say so to her mother, there was no way Liz was going down that painful road again. Lessons learned the first time around didn't have to be repeated, and Andrew had certainly taught her to keep her heart closed.

"Your father sends his love."

The muscles in Liz's neck and shoulders tightened so suddenly, so painfully she almost gasped aloud. Instead, she pressed her lips together for an instant and clenched her fingers around the cup. When she replied, it was years of practice that allowed her to keep her tone level.

"Tell him I said hello."

It was the best that she could do right now. The wounds were still too fresh, her sense of betrayal still too painful for anything more.

"Eliza..."

But that was all her mother said, and the silence stretched between them, filled with the ghosts of past mistakes and family secrets too long hidden. Liz wasn't surprised by her mother's inability to articulate whatever it was she wanted to say. Heart-to-hearts and speaking about emotional subjects weren't "done" in their family.

Things might be a damned sight better if they were but, after all these years, they wouldn't know where to start.

She was gripping the phone so hard her fingers were beginning to ache, mirroring the pain in her suddenly roiling stomach. She didn't have time for this. Not right now. Probably never.

"I have to get back inside, Mother. I'm still on duty. I'm glad you enjoyed your trip."

"Thank you, dear." Her mother spoke softly, almost wistfully, and Liz wondered if she, like her daughter, wished things could go back to the way they used to be. "We'll talk again soon."

Disconnecting the call, Liz thrust the phone into the pocket of her coat and turned her face up toward the murky sky, taking a deep breath, trying to relax.

It was actually funny, in a twisted type of way. She'd always been an outsider in the family, set apart. While she loved her parents, she'd often felt emotionally distant from them, while Robbie, three years her junior, had been the affectionate one, the glue holding the family together. The fact that he was adopted hadn't mattered. She'd been too young when he'd arrived to care, and had loved him, unconditionally, ever since.

Perhaps it was the thought of settling down with Giovanna and starting a family of his own that had prompted Robbie to ask for information about his biological parents. Whatever the reason, neither he nor Liz had been prepared for the answer, delivered one summer's evening last year while the family had spent a couple of days together at the beach house.

Robbie was Brant Prudhomme's biological son, conceived when Brant had had an affair not long after Liz's birth.

"We went through a bad patch," Lorelei had said, her still-beautiful face pale, her eyes damp. "But, in the end, we decided to make it work. And when Brant told me Robbie's mother was dying…"

"Your mother is a wonderful woman," Brant had interjected, in the tone Liz had known from experience meant the conversation was all but over. "I don't think either of you would argue that point."

Too stunned to say anything, or ask questions, Liz had watched her father walk out of the room, his back stiff and straight. Lorelei had looked suddenly more fragile but, as usual, it had been Robbie who'd gone to her, hugged her, and reassured her everything would be fine.

Liz hadn't shared his optimism. From that moment, her world had felt off kilter, and she doubted it would ever be completely put back to rights again. Knowing that her father, who Liz would have sworn was a good husband, had betrayed her mother's trust like that had devastated her.

What little faith she'd had in men had practically been destroyed.

Since that day, anger had lain like a rock in her chest. Why the situation affected her this way was something she was loath to look at too closely. All she knew was she couldn't deal with being around or speaking to her father yet. Maybe the anger would fade over time and she'd relent, but not yet. Sometimes that anger spilled over to her mother too, but Lorelei, for all her bustle and chattiness, had somehow always struck Liz as being in need of protection. Being careful not to let her know the extent of the rage her daughter felt was important.

Suddenly realizing her face tingled from the cold, Liz took one last deep breath and twisted her head from side to side, trying to work out the stiffness in her muscles. It was time to get back to work, to lose herself in the job she loved more than anything else in the world, at the hospital that held a special place in her heart.

Liz's great-grandfather had been one of the founding fathers of Hepplewhite General, which eventually had been named after him. When she'd completed her residency and applied there she hadn't revealed her connection to the hospital, which had made winning the position that much more satisfying.

She was sure that somewhere, in the afterlife, her great-aunts had chuckled.

Her Great-Aunt Honoria had wanted to study medicine, but her father had refused to allow it. And when Liz's father had expressed reservations about his daughter going into what he'd described as "a grueling, heartbreaking profession" Honoria and her sister, Eliza, had paid for her schooling.

"Do what you want in life," Aunt Honoria had said. "Be useful, and don't allow your father, or any man, to dictate to you. Eliza and I wish we'd had the courage to do that ourselves."

The advice had been sound, and in line with what her nursemaid, Nanny Hardy, had taught her as a child. Heeding their collective guidance had led to her success, while the one time she'd not followed it had led to disaster and heartbreak.

No, she loved her work and Hepplewhite, with its associations with the past, and had made it the main focus of her life. Never had she been more grateful for how busy the ER kept her than now.

There was nothing like a full workload to keep the chaotic thoughts at bay. This winter had seen a particularly active flu season, still in full swing, and with the waves of snowstorms hitting New York City had come an uptick of heart attacks, slip-and-fall injuries and the like. The hospital staff wasn't immune to the flu either, and there were a few out sick, which increased everyone's workload.

As she swiped her badge to open the door, Liz's stomach rumbled. She'd been heading for the cafeteria a couple hours ago when a commotion in the ER waiting area had caught her attention. Four clearly frightened young men had been at the intake desk, supporting a fifth who'd appeared to be unconscious and bleeding from a facial wound. They had all been talking at once.

"He fell—"

"Momma's gonna kill us—"

"He won't wake up—"

Lunch forgotten, Liz had grabbed a nearby gurney and hit the electronic door opener, not waiting for an orderly. Even from a distance she had been able to see the youngster had needed immediate treatment.

As it turned out, the teens had cut school and somehow found their way past the protective fencing surrounding the hospital's ongoing construction project. Once there, her patient decided to use the equipment and building rubble to practice his parkour skills. Probably not the best of ideas, given the slick of ice that still covered some surfaces. It had cost him a broken jaw, a concussion and the kind of laceration that, without plastic surgery, would leave a disfiguring scar.

By the time she'd examined him, made sure he was stable and sent for the oral and plastic surgeons, she'd only had another two and a half hours before her twelve-hour shift would be finished. Rather than bother with a break, and cognizant of the full waiting room, she'd only taken enough time to call her mother.

Striding down the corridor toward the ER, Liz put her family drama, and its attendant pain, aside. There was no place for it here in the hospital, where all her attention had to be on her patients' well-being.

That was what was truly important.

On the way home she'd stop at her favorite diner and treat herself to an everything omelet with home fries. Just the thought made her mouth water and her stomach rumble again.

CHAPTER TWO

AFTER TAKING OFF her coat and making her way back to the ER, Liz noticed a certain buzz in the air that hadn't been there before she'd gone outside. Before she could ask one of the other doctors what was going on, she was called away to deal with a patient brought in by ambulance.

Paramedics had received a report of a man acting irrationally and, on arrival, had found Mr. Josiah Collins combative and uncooperative, with a severe laceration on his arm. Although they also said he'd calmed down quickly, and there'd been no problems with him since, there was something about the man's watchful quiescence and refusal to give much information that had Liz on high alert.

She ordered blood tests, and stitched the laceration. Then, signaling to one of the nurses to join her, she stepped out and walked a few paces along the corridor leading to the ER nurses' station.

"Put a rush on those samples. I need those results, stat, so I can know whether he's on something or is just having a psychotic break. And have one of the security personnel keep an eye on him, please."

"Yes Dr. Prudhomme."

The nurse immediately started off, but paused as Liz said, "And, Stella? Nice job on that thoracotomy patient earlier. I appreciate it."

With a smile and a nod of acknowledgement, Stella went on her way, and Liz walked toward the nurses' station.

There was no need for her to elaborate. Stella knew to what she was referring. The patient had been awake, alert and in extreme pain. Taking advantage of the brief thaw, he'd been working on a roof and slipped, the fall causing chest trauma and fractures to both arms and one leg. Already distressed, he'd grown more distraught as a massive hemothorax had caused blood to fill his chest cavity, compressing his lungs and making breathing increasingly difficult.

Inserting a chest tube was a great deal easier to do when the patient was unconscious and Liz had been prepared to have a difficult time of it until Stella, with impeccable timing, had distracted the patient, held his attention and kept him calm through the painful procedure. Stella's intuition and ability to connect quickly and effectively with the patient deserved acknowledgement.

Liz was more than aware of her own shortcomings in the human interaction arena. Her lack of affectionate gestures, her cool contemplation of, and reaction to, life had been pointed out repeatedly, and not as positive traits. She wasn't into giving constant praise for every little thing. They all had their jobs to do, from the ER doctors and trauma surgeons to the orderlies. She didn't expect congratulations for every correct diagnosis she made or course of treatment she set in motion, and neither should anyone else for doing their job.

However, she also knew her reputation was one of a hard-assed, unsmiling witch. It was true, and she had no complaints on that score. However, just because she didn't make nice with everyone, it didn't mean she didn't care about the people she worked with.

It was just simpler not to care *too* much, not build friendships and relationships that could, potentially, interfere with her job. She already had close friends from her university days. Although they were now scattered across the globe, Liz really didn't see any need to make new ones.

She was heading to the nurses' station to get a jump on her charting when she was interrupted by a nurse informing her that her young parkour patient's mother had arrived, and was in the waiting room.

Her stomach rumbled again, reminding her she'd been on duty for eleven and a half hours and hadn't ingested anything more than a couple of energy bars and half a cup of coffee. It was just one of those days.

Micah Johnston's mother was by turns livid at her son and scared about his prognosis, and it took some time to calm her down. As soon as she'd escorted the lady to her son's cubicle to speak to the surgeons, Liz strode purposefully once more toward the nearest nurses' station.

She really had to get her charting done ASAP, so maybe, just maybe, she could leave the hospital on time and stop her stomach from devouring itself.

"Ah, there she is. Liz, a moment please."

Damn it!

She turned toward Gregory Hammond's voice,

biting back a growl of annoyance at being way-laid once more. Luckily she'd assumed a politely questioning expression because, as she looked at the man walking next to the chief of surgery, her face, along with the rest of her body, froze.

There was no mistaking his carriage, the set of his head, the clear-cut features of the man she'd had a glorious one-night stand with in Mexico. To suddenly see him again, when she'd thought she never would, made her head feel light and her legs weak.

How could she not recognize him? First off, he was tall. Tall enough that she, five-ten in her stockinged feet, had to look up at him, a rarity indeed, and he carried himself with easy assurance, his back militarily straight, his strides long and strong.

Second, although she wouldn't classify him as handsome, there was something compelling about his face. It was wide, with a prominent nose and deep-set, hooded eyes. A firm chin and mouth rounded out the picture. From a distance she'd been attracted, but it was seeing him up close that had cemented her interest. His eyes were spectacular. Dark amber in the center, shading to brown around the edge of the iris, they were serious and hinted at the kind of intelligence Liz always found appealing.

Heat rushed from her toes to the top of her head as her gaze was captured and transfixed by those unforgettable eyes, partially masked behind lowered lids. They gleamed, and she wasn't sure what the glint in them was. Anger? Annoyance? Amusement?

Her heart went into overdrive, a mixture of irritation and mortification rushing through her in an instant.

Then all the years of training drummed into her by her mother and tutors arose to come to her rescue. Inner heat was replaced by cold tension, but she refused to allow it to show. Straightening her back and lifting her chin, she tore her gaze away from his companion and gratefully turned her attention to Gregory Hammond.

"Liz, I want you to meet our newest trauma surgeon, Dr. Cort Smith. Dr. Smith, this is Dr. Liz Prudhomme, one of our fine ER practitioners."

Politeness dictated she look at Dr. Smith again, but it took considerable effort to make herself do it. Her brain was racing as fast as her heart, wondering if he was about to say they'd already met; if somehow he would make it clear their involvement had been of the intimate kind.

There were plenty of men who wouldn't be able to resist doing so, just to up their reputations as ladies' men.

But Cort Smith just stuck out his hand and said, politely, "How do you do, Dr. Prudhomme?"

Just the sound of that deep voice, so familiar and arousing, made her wish she were a hundred miles away. How could he be so cool, while she wanted to run for the hills? It was tempting to focus on his Adam's apple or chin, rather than meet those compelling eyes again, but that would be the coward's way out, so she met his gaze with what she hoped was a calm one of her own.

"Very well, thank you," she replied, as she took his hand. A *zing* of electricity rushed up her arm, and she tugged her hand away as swiftly as she could without being rude.

The corners of Cort Smith's mouth twitched, making Liz want to smack him.

"Dr. Smith starts his first full day tomorrow," Gregory said. He seemed oblivious to the tension swirling between herself and Cort, which Liz swore was so thick she could taste it. "I hope you'll take whatever time is necessary to point him in the right direction while he gets settled."

She'd point him right out the door, if she had her way! But Liz only nodded, and decided the politic answer was best. "Of course."

Thankfully, before the voluble Gregory could get chatting again, Stella interrupted.

"Dr. Prudhomme, I have the lab reports on Mr. Collins."

"Thank you." Her relief was almost strong enough to make her smile, but not quite. With a quick, "If you gentlemen will excuse me," she hightailed it away as fast as she could without actually running.

Why did it feel as though the universe had decided her previously nice, orderly existence was too good to be true, and was throwing her curveballs left, right and center?

Cort watched Liz Prudhomme walk away, amazed at how unruffled she'd been by a meeting he'd found hard to face with aplomb. Besides a reddening of the tips of her ears when she'd turned and seen him, there had been no other discernible reaction to show she'd even recognized him.

After he'd caught sight of her at the door earlier, he'd tried to convince himself it wasn't really the woman he'd spent the night with in Mexico. For the last seven months he'd been so hung up on the memory of that encounter he'd dreamt about her almost constantly, and had thought, erroneously, he'd glimpsed her in crowds at least a hundred times.

And she looked different, with her brown hair pulled back into a simple ponytail instead of in a sleek bob to below her chin. The streak of aqua she'd had framing one side of her face was gone too, but they were definitely the same strong features he'd committed to memory. Those mesmerizing, mossy-green eyes, almond-shaped and thick-lashed, had the same steady, controlled gaze that had attracted him before.

She wouldn't be classified as beautiful by most people's standards. Tall, solidly built, with strong shoulders and wide hips, she was anything but model skinny. From a distance, she would seem the perfect fit for the girl next door, or the sidekick in a romantic movie. But once a person saw her up close, Cort knew they couldn't see her in either role.

Her face was too strong, with high cheekbones,

lips a trifle thinner than were fashionable, and a chin that hinted at a stubborn, willful nature. Here was a woman unused and unwilling to bend and, although he admired strength of character, he'd always been attracted to a softer type. Until the night they'd slept together, and she'd proved strength when yielded for desire brought more pleasure than he'd ever imagined.

Yet even if he'd still been unsure whether it was her or not, once he heard her speak there could be no question. Despite its careful control, her voice was still rich and decadent, like Cherries Jubilee without the brandy burnt off, and hearing it had made goose bumps race along his spine. Realizing it absolutely was her had filled him with a mixture of disbelief, horror and unwanted excitement. Life would be a lot simpler if she'd stayed just a memory and attendant fantasy, not a flesh-and-blood person he had to work with.

And always remember how she'd run out on him that night without a word.

"Liz is a fine practitioner. One of our best diagnosticians," Gregory was saying. "And although some of the staff seem to find her rather standoffish, we've never had any complaints from patients about either her standard of care or bedside manner."

Standoffish? He could only hope she would be standoffish with him too. Against his will and best intentions, already the memory of having her, flushed and damp with pleasure in his bed was threatening to push everything else out of his head.

"And I have to warn you she will not stand for any nonsense when it comes to proper protocol." Gregory started walking again, and Cort fell in beside him. "Not that she should, you understand, but she's particularly unforgiving when it comes to our surgeons overstepping their boundaries."

Ah, so she was at least one of the sources of the "friction" Dr. Hammond had spoken of earlier. He was searching for the correct way to ask for more information when a howling cry arose from down the hall. It was followed swiftly by a metallic crash and a shout. Instinct had Cort running toward the noise, following Liz as she disappeared, also at a run, around a corner.

She was closer to the commotion, but he had the advantage of longer legs, so he was only two steps behind her when she dashed into one of the cubicles.

Everything seemed to slow down, allowing him to take in the large man thrashing about on the bed, a security guard struggling to restrain him. Liz sprang forward just as the patient's arm swung back, and Cort bit back a curse, knowing he was too far away to stop her from getting hit...

Liz twisted away from the flailing fist, the move so graceful and efficient Cort could hardly believe it, then she grabbed the patient's wrist.

The man went rigid, all the fight going out of him, as though Liz's touch sucked it away. The guard quickly secured one wrist with a restraint cuff while Liz secured the other, and Cort got to work putting ankle belts in place, assisted by a nurse who'd come in behind him.

"I know you're frightened." Patient secured, Liz leaned over him, spoke to him with what Cort recognized from their time together in Mexico as habitual directness. There wasn't a hint of stress in her voice, and Cort, whose system still hummed with adrenaline, mentally shook his head at her cool. "But we're going to help you."

Cort backed out of the room as Liz started

giving orders to the nurses. He wasn't even supposed to be there, and he wondered if he'd already earned a strike with her, given her strictness on protocol.

Dr. Hammond was down the hall, speaking into his phone again, so Cort waited outside the patient's cubicle for Liz to come out. Might as well take whatever she had to say on the chin and apologize if necessary, rather than let it fester or have her formally complain.

When she stepped out of the room she paused, allowing the nurses to pass them before she spoke.

"It wasn't necessary for you to jump in like that. We have exceptionally well-trained staff here, and rushing to the rescue every time there's a hint of excitement isn't within your purview."

He shrugged, and stuck his hands in the pockets of his lab coat, annoyed once more at how unconcerned she was about seeing him again. He felt as though there was an eggbeater running amok in his stomach. "It was instinct. The sound of a fight and a kidney dish hitting the floor will always bring me running." She'd warned him off clearly: the patient inside that room had nothing to do with him. So, just to needle her, he asked, "Do you have a diagnosis?"

The look she gave him was level, but he was sure there was a flash of annoyance behind her veiled glance. Which was why he was surprised when, after a moment, she actually replied.

"Just got the labs back. There are trace amounts of clozapine in his system. I think he stopped taking his medication and is having a schizophrenic episode. The psych team is on its way down." Her gaze dared him to express an opinion, and he figured it was time to change the subject, even before she added, with a touch of ice in her tone, "Nothing more either of us can do right now."

If he hadn't figured it out before, now he knew for sure. Dr. Liz Prudhomme was as tough as rebar and cooler than a mountain spring. Yet under that realization was the still clear image of her in Mexico, vulnerable to his every touch. It took every ounce of willpower to lock the memory away again. He had to deal with her simply as a new colleague, a potentially difficult one at that, in the place he'd chosen to start over. Whatever had happened between them in the honeymoon suite in Mexico had no bearing on the here and now. Yet he felt he owed it to himself, and to her, to clear the air.

"Listen." Cort lowered his voice. "I wasn't sure you'd want anyone to know we'd met before. I was trying to be discreet."

"That's fine." The steady gaze didn't waver, but the ice in her voice was solid now. "I keep my private life private, so I... I actually appreciate it."

That little hesitation tugged at his chest, although he wasn't sure why. Perhaps it had something to do with its incongruity, given her air of total confidence. Without thought, he said, "Well, I'd rather the staff here didn't know I'd been dumped right before my wedding too, so being discreet is pretty easy for me."

She didn't reply, except with a lift of her eyebrows and a sideways tilt of her head, which he interpreted as a dismissive gesture, before she turned to walk away. He should leave it at that, yet the urge to keep hearing that Cherries Jubilee voice was hard to ignore, no matter how aggravating she was.

She was already a few strides down the hall when he called after her, "What was that wrist lock you used? Aikido?"

That brought her up short, and those telling eyebrows rose again as she paused and looked back at him. "Hapkido. You're a martial artist?"

"Used to be, full on, until I got accepted into med school. Kept involved while I was in the army too." He held out his hands and flexed his fingers. "But I've stopped sparring, since I don't want to break anything, although that didn't end my fascination."

For a moment she didn't reply, seemed to be staring at his hands, then she looked back up at him. "Huh. Wimp."

Wow, she didn't pull any punches, did she? But he couldn't help the smile tugging at his lips. "Want to test that hypothesis sometime?"

Liz just shook her head, but the corner of her mouth twitched. "I'd kick your butt."

"No doubt," he replied, making no attempt to stop her this time when she moved away. "I've no doubt at all."

And it occurred to him, as he watched that delectable body disappear around the corner, she could do a great deal more than just kick his butt physically.

If he was stupid enough to let her.

CHAPTER THREE

"I SHOT HIM," the patient moaned, her voice distorted not just by the oxygen mask but also her severe facial injuries. "I shot him."

It was all she'd said since she'd been brought in, over and over again, no matter what Liz asked her. She'd barely reacted to any of the procedures they'd done to try to stabilize her condition, despite the additional pain they must have caused her.

"Kaitlin, where hurts the most?"

"I shot him. I shot him."

"Any word from Trauma?" Liz asked the room at large.

"I'm here."

Cort Smith dumped a bloody surgical gown into the bin by the door, and paused to drag on a fresh one. "What do we have?"

Even as focused as she was on her patient, Liz's heart did a little dip when she heard his voice.

I'll get used to having him around.

That was what Liz had been telling herself repeatedly since the day Cort strode back into her life but, a month on, she still had a visceral reaction every time she saw him. Having to work with him presented another layer to her problem, since she found herself sometimes having to fight to concentrate.

The movements of his hands, the calm, soothing quality of his deep voice when he spoke to patients, did things to her insides. They brought to mind the way he'd touched her so masterfully as he'd murmured in her ear that night so long ago, telling her to come.

It was extremely annoying and she once more resolved to ignore it. The badly beaten and stabbed woman in front of her deserved all her concentration.

"Twenty-four-year-old Kaitlin Hayle, facial trauma and multiple penetrating wounds to thorax and abdomen, both anterior and posterior. Limited lung sounds on the right when brought in; chest tube inserted."

As she continued to bring him up to speed, she chafed at the delay having to do so caused. It was information she'd already transmitted to

Dr. Yuen, and she was surprised that Cort had attended. Normally the doctor she'd spoken to initially would be the one to come down. Something had caused the change in procedure, and therefore the delay, and she wasn't happy about it.

One thing Liz could readily admit to with Dr. Smith, though, was how thorough he was.

"Hey, Kaitlin," he said, in that deep, calm voice, while checking her pupils. "My name is Dr. Smith. I'm going to be examining you, okay?"

"I shot him."

Cort continued his methodical examination, working his way down to the two penetrating wounds on Kaitlin's thorax.

"They look to be at least two inches deep," Liz said, as he started palpating the area around the first wound. "And that one seems to angle downward."

Having examined both the anterior wounds, he merely said, "Roll her," so he could examine the posterior one.

Once he was through, he moved back to the head of the table and leaned over the patient.

"Kaitlin, I'm going to have to operate. You have internal injuries that have to be repaired. We'll take good care of you, okay?"

Kaitlin's gaze flickered to Cort's face, and stayed there for a moment. Then, surprisingly, she said, "Okay. Okay."

"Good girl," he replied, giving her shoulder a quick squeeze.

The shock must be wearing off, thanks to the drip, Liz thought a little sourly. How else to explain his ability to get through to their patient when she hadn't been able to at all?

With a little jerk of his head, Cort beckoned Liz to the far side of the room, out of Kaitlin's earshot.

"I want her to have a CT scan before I go in. She seems stable enough to take the time, and I'll have a better idea of what I'm facing before I open her up."

"I'll call up to Radiology right now," Liz replied. "And I'll go up with her."

"Thanks." He gave her a half smile. "I'll keep an eye on her vitals while you're gone."

As she turned away to go to the phone, Liz was annoyed with herself all over again.

Why was it his smiles, even half ones, made her want to smile back? She wasn't the smiling type at all, and yet something about him made her almost wish she were.

She'd been careful to keep him firmly at arm's length and act with the utmost professionalism toward him, determined to eventually exorcise the hyperawareness she experienced around him. It was aggravating in the extreme that the rest of the Hepplewhite staff seemed equally determined to keep Cort in the center of the gossip mill, and she could hardly move without hearing someone say his name.

Just that morning, when she'd been in the line at the cafeteria, there had been a couple of nurses in front of her talking about him, as though there was nothing else of any interest to chat about.

"He's been here for a while, what have you been able to find out about him?"

Liz knew who Marcie was talking about even before Trisha answered.

"Nothing but what I was able to find in the Cramer General website archives. Served in the army and got his training through it. Honorably discharged about five years ago and went straight to Cramer."

"That's it? Do we even know if he's married or not?"

Trisha shook her head, disgruntlement clear in her tone when she replied, "He's real nice, but a clam when it comes to talking about himself."

"Even with you, Miss Southern Charm?" Marcie snickered. "I'm surprised you don't have him spilling his guts over some sweet potato pie and a mint julep."

"Ha-ha-ha," Trisha replied, as she elbowed her friend and they both laughed.

Liz too was surprised that Trisha hadn't had any luck. The nurse was petite, almost elfin, with the most beautiful dark mocha complexion and the face of an angel. Plus, she had the kind of voice Liz remembered, as a teen, wishing she had. It was as sweet and light as fresh whipped cream, not low and raspy, like its owner subsisted on a diet of rusty nails and rye whiskey. Mind you, a voice like Trisha's would sound pretty stupid coming from her, who was almost a foot taller and nowhere near petite.

As she relayed Cort's request to Radiology, she resolved once more do something about how often she thought about him, dreamed about being with him in Mexico. She was loath to admit it, even to herself, but he'd turned her inside out that night, given her an experience she'd never had before.

Maybe because of her forthright nature, men seemed to assume she'd be demanding in bed and, since it was the best way to get the satisfaction she deserved, she usually was. However, Cort Smith had taken masterful control of her body, coaxing her to new erotic heights and making her have to reevaluate what it was she truly desired. When she'd snuck out of his room in the early hours of the morning, it hadn't just been because she'd had a flight to catch. She'd been awash in pleasure so intense as to be frightening.

There was no secret enjoyment in the fact she knew more about the sexy doctor than anyone else at the hospital. Intimate facts that still made her skin heat and her libido go through the roof. Instead, the knowledge she possessed just made working with him harder. Trying to view him just as a colleague was difficult in the extreme, but she was determined to do just that.

Hopefully, the more she had to interact with him, the more likely the annoying attraction she still felt would wither away.

* * *

"There." Cort pointed to where the CT images of Kaitlin's body were on the screen. "Definite laceration to the liver. And…" He was aware of Liz leaning closer, her attention focused on the movement of his finger, and for a split second lost his train of thought.

"Is that fluid around the stomach?" she asked.

"And air," he replied, pulling himself together. He was about to operate to try to save a young woman's life. There was no time for loss of concentration, no matter the source. What he was seeing on the CT scan indicated the internal injuries were probably quite extensive.

And they were. What he had estimated would be an hour-long operation stretched to two and a half hours, as he discovered Kaitlin's diaphragm and stomach, as well as her liver, had been damaged. As he cauterized and stitched, he reflected on how lucky the young woman had been.

He wasn't really surprised to come out of surgery and see Liz waiting to hear the outcome. Yet as he took a few moments to take off his surgical gear and wash up, his awareness of her just on the other side of the doors was disconcerting.

Settling in at Hepplewhite, in New York City

itself, had been difficult enough, but every time he came into contact with Dr. Liz Prudhomme it intensified his sense of disorientation. Which was funny, in a weird rather than amusing sort of way, since it was something she'd said to him in Mexico that had prompted his move from Colorado.

Although they'd just met, he'd found himself telling her about being jilted only weeks before the wedding. What she'd said to him had lingered in his mind.

Sometimes, when life seems to be screwed up, you need to take a chance on the change that's been forced on you, you know? Figure out what it would take to make the crappy stuff into an asset, or a benefit. Maybe you've had a lucky escape, being dumped. I don't know, but now's the time for you to make a new, better plan. That's what I do when life tries to mess with me, anyway.

On reflection, her advice had made perfect sense. Wasn't he the poster child for overcoming? For taking whatever effluvium life flung at him and making something worthwhile out of it? In comparison to all he'd been through, being jilted was, in the final analysis, insignificant. It was nothing when weighed against being abandoned as a baby, surviving the foster-care system, or losing his best friend. It was even small potatoes when compared to the depression that had blanketed him following Brody's death. What it had done, though, was underscore how much he'd been drifting along through life.

The job at Cramer had been a sound choice, given his desire to be close to Jenna and the kids, and, although demanding, strangely easy after being deployed. He'd done well but after Mimi's defection had decided to reactivate his childhood wish to travel the world, get to know new places intimately, before moving on to the next. And where better to start than in New York City?

It had seemed a perfect plan, until he'd found himself working with Liz Prudhomme and had realized he'd not just made a change but turned his entire life upside down.

He couldn't make her out.

While he'd never heard her be rude, there was a distance between her and the world, a wall created of solemn, clear-eyed looks and cool professionalism. Although being the epitome of calm whenever they worked together, occasionally she'd glance at him, and all the arousal he tried to suppress rushed through him anew. For him, the spirit of the woman he'd had in his bed hovered in the back of his mind continually. A ghostly fantasy, flushed and excited, her body bowing and twisting with ecstasy yearned for and then achieved.

He'd give anything to be rid of those memories and the fantasies they inspired, but not even seeing her in her usual milieu, which was anything but sexy, helped.

If anything, it made her more fascinating. Every time he met those clear green eyes, or saw her striding purposefully through the hospital, it enticed him further.

Apparently, along with all his other issues, he was a masochist too. If that weren't the case, surely it would be easy to push aside the attraction he still felt? And it wasn't just the sexual appeal either. Something about that self-containment of hers interested him. Maybe in it he saw an echo of his own distance from others, and couldn't help wondering where hers sprang from.

Whatever the reasons, it made dealing with her a constant strain, and now he wished she'd simply called up to the surgical floor to find out how the operation had gone, rather than waiting around. With a sigh of resignation he pushed through the doors into the corridor beyond.

She was in street clothes, a pair of jeans that fit her curves perfectly and a coral sweater that somehow made her skin glow. A handbag, the size of a small suitcase, was on her shoulder, and she carried her winter jacket over one arm. Apparently she was about to go home.

"How did it go?" she asked, with habitual directness.

"Pretty well," he replied, before giving her a more detailed account of the injuries he'd found and repaired. "I think she'll make a full recovery."

Liz glanced down the hall, toward the waiting area. "The police are waiting to speak to her. Apparently, she did shoot her boyfriend. I didn't realize he'd been brought in too, not long before she was."

Cort nodded. "Initially I was treating him, and then Dr. Hammond told Dr. Yuen to take over and sent me down to attend on Kaitlin."

Dr. Yuen was young, newly licensed and not as experienced as Cort with the types of multiple injuries Kaitlin had experienced. The younger doctor had seemed nonplussed to have been pulled away from such an interesting case, but what the chief of surgery decreed went.

Liz's face tightened for an instant, then smoothed out again. "Well, the boyfriend survived, and is telling the cops she shot him, and he was just defending himself when he beat and stabbed her. It'll be interesting to see how it all pans out."

"I'll let you know if I hear anything," he said. "It'll probably take a while for the cops to figure it out."

Liz nodded, turning on her heel. "Thanks. I'm on my way out, so I'll see you."

"See you," he replied to her retreating back, leaving him watching the enticing sway of her hips for a few moments before he caught himself and went to talk to the police.

CHAPTER FOUR

CORT WAS JUST doing his job, Liz thought sourly a week later, but that didn't stop her wishing he was doing it somewhere else. No matter his intent, his presence sure didn't improve productivity in the ER department.

She was sitting at a computer, doing some research, when Cort came down to speak to one of the other physicians about a case. It was slower in the department. While the emergency room was being revamped and expanded, there was less traffic, with more serious cases being routed to other hospitals in the area. Cort had been asked to take on more general surgery cases until things picked up again, and had apparently agreed without demurring. Right now he was consulting with Dr. Durham and a steady stream of nurses was coming by, each one lingering for what Liz considered to be an unconscionable time within gawking range.

He was a menace!

And why was he hanging about so long too? Surely he had rounds to do up on the surgical floor?

Yet all the gossip she'd heard about him so far was still of the glowing variety, not even counting the comments about his looks. The nurses loved him, had no complaints about either the way he handled his patients or how he dealt with staff, and they were usually the first to grumble and moan about the surgeons. Her own co-workers in the ER department also seemed happy with how he interacted with them. Even Durham, the crankiest of them all, was right at this very minute grinning like a demented fool at Cort Smith.

Mind you, it was fairly rare to find a surgeon who was content to take a wait-and-see approach when the patient might, in the end, still need an op. From the conversation going on between Durham and Smith, that was exactly the situation they were discussing. Keeping her gaze on the screen in front of her didn't stop her from listening in.

"I'll be going off shift in about twenty minutes," Cort said. "But if Mrs. McClacken's obstruction doesn't sort itself out, I've briefed Dr. Morrison, and he's prepared to do the operation."

Durham snorted, his version of a laugh. "She'll be disappointed you're not operating."

Liz wanted to snort too, but not with laughter. She was too exhausted to find it funny, and blamed her sleepless nights squarely on Cort Smith. It was all too ridiculous, like working with a blasted rock star, having him around. Everyone wanted a piece of him. Not her, though, she reminded herself stoutly, despite the memories that had her tossing and turning at night, equal parts aroused and furious. It made having to see him every day a torment.

Worse, his easygoing manner and smiling demeanor reminded her of Andrew. Charming, lovable Andrew, who'd had everyone falling over themselves to please him, even Liz. But what he'd wanted from her had been so much more than she'd been able to give. He'd complained she wasn't affectionate enough, and the memory of being told she was too cold and controlled for him still stung all these years later.

It wasn't that she hadn't loved him. She had, so much so that she had been tempted, when he'd asked, to give up her studies and travel with him in Europe. Yet, in the end, Andrew had broken her heart and gone off on his own, preferring adventure to a life with her, and leaving her to pick up the pieces of her life the best way she could. There had been a corner of her heart still hoping he would come back, say he'd been wrong and she was all he'd ever need, but it hadn't happened. Would never happen as, before they'd been able to mend the rift, he'd been killed in a motorcycle accident in Germany.

Durham had gone but now one of the nurses was asking Cort something, gazing up at him as though she'd just discovered religion and it was the Church of Smith. It was the same way women of all ages had stared at Andrew, and the similarity made Liz's stomach clench.

Forcing her gaze back down to the monitor, she tried to push aside the painful thoughts, but one thing remained clear. Staying away from Cort Smith as much as possible was the very best thing she could do, for her sanity, if nothing else.

"Excuse me, Dr. Prudhomme."

Liz looked up on hearing her name, but didn't recognize the young man standing beside her. "Yes?"

"Mrs. Lister, in HR, asked me to let you know

that there are some changes being made to the credential verification process. She noticed it's been over nine months since your trip to Mexico and, since you tend to go on a medical mission trip once a year, she wanted you to be aware of the changes."

In her peripheral vision, she noticed Cort's head turn, as though he were looking at her, and she knew the mention of Mexico had attracted his attention. Her toes curled in her sneakers, heat bloomed in her belly, and it took all her concentration not to glance his way. Just the mention of her trip threatened to overwhelm her with all the memories she was trying so hard to suppress.

"Oh, thanks." She kept her voice level and her focus on the man in front of her. "Could you tell Mrs. Lister I don't have a trip planned right now, but ask her to email me the new protocol so I have it on hand?"

"Sure, Dr. Prudhomme."

As he walked away, she turned her attention back to the website on myasthenia gravis. Committing to memory the information she wanted, she signed out of the system, but before she could get up, her cell phone pinged with an incoming text message, and she took it out to look.

Robbie, reminding her about her promise to attend a fundraising luncheon in his place the following day, since he was in London with Giovanna.

It made her annoyance peak.

When her great-aunts had left the majority of their wealth in a philanthropic fund and had named Liz as the trustee, she'd balked at the responsibility. Yet she owed them a debt and had known she couldn't refuse. Not only had they funded her schooling without hesitation, they'd also been a refuge for her, stalwart in their support of her ambitions when her parents had tried to talk her out of pursuing a medical career.

As a compromise, Robbie had agreed to sit on the board and become the face of the trust, which had made sense, since his financial contacts and experience would be invaluable. Not to mention how much more easily he mixed and mingled in the high social circles her family frequented.

But he was all caught up in the preparations for his wedding and, not unreasonably, wanted to spend as much time as possible with Giovanna. London Fashion Week was about to start, and he'd promised to be there while his fiancée modeled for a new, haute couture designer. Liz didn't blame him, but having to dress up and press the flesh while talking about nonprofits, investments and the like wasn't anywhere near the top of her favorite things list.

More like at the bottom.

Shoving her phone into her pocket, she tried not to look, but found her gaze drawn straight back to Cort. He was still listening to the nurse, but his attention was on Liz, and she couldn't help wondering if he, like her, had been drawn back into thoughts of their night together.

Dragging her gaze away from his, she got up. There were patients waiting for her, and putting some distance between her and Cort would be a very good thing just then. Liz pushed in her chair and had only taken a couple of steps when a nurse called out.

"Incoming baby, found in a dumpster. Hypothermic, unresponsive. Cops aren't waiting for the ambulance. They're bringing it in themselves."

Immediately Liz was moving, training taking over. With a glance at the board, she barked, "Room two. Sanjay, heat lamp and thermal blankets. Marion, warm saline and an oxygen hood.

Jessica, call up to Pediatrics and have them on standby."

Then, as she set off at a run for the ambulance bay, she realized Cort was ahead of her, rushing to meet the incoming police car as though he were wearing a cape and only he could save the patient.

Oh, hell, no.

This was the kind of usurpation that shouldn't be allowed. There was absolutely no reason for him to be involved, and she didn't care if it was an instinctive reaction to hearing it was a child coming in. He couldn't be allowed to overreach his purview. Not on her watch.

He was sprinting toward the intake door and, with a burst of speed, she caught up to him just as he was going through it. The cold slapped her face, hard, stealing her breath for a moment, but then, with the sound of sirens screaming closer, she came up beside him. As she pulled on a pair of gloves, she said in her firmest voice, "Dr. Smith, you're not—"

Cort Smith turned and glanced down at her, and whatever she was planning to say next caught in her suddenly bone-dry throat.

There was an expression on his face she'd

never seen before, and yet instinctively recognized. The blank stare spoke of hyper-focus, the tightness of mouth and jaw heralded not an unwillingness to yield but an inability. Curling her fingers into fists so tight she could feel her short nails through her gloves, she realized the futility of trying to block him from treating the child.

He turned away as the police car fishtailed on the thin slick of snow at the entrance to the bay, dismissing her, and Liz took a calming breath.

Later. She'd take him to task later.

The police car's front passenger door flew open even before the vehicle came to a complete stop, and a burly officer swung out. He looked to be hugging himself, holding his winter jacket closed as the wind caught the edge of the emergency blanket hanging down from below the edge of the coat, making it crackle and shimmer in the harsh lights.

Cort didn't try to take the child out of its warm cocoon but rushed the officer into the hospital.

"Room two," Liz called out, a step behind them.

"Homeless guy said he heard a noise from inside the dumpster, fished the baby out while someone called us." Even though he was running, the officer's voice was steady, factual. "Took us three minutes to get to the scene from the time the call came in. I thought I felt a pulse when we first got there, but there's been no movement or sound since. I think it's a newborn, but I'm not sure."

Cort swung through the door, guiding the officer, and Liz made no attempt to take the child, knowing Cort would do it, compelled as he was by some unknown force to take the lead. Instead, she moved quickly to the far side of the examination table, looking for the position of the heat lamp, making sure everything she needed was in place.

Cort unwrapped the child from the emergency blanket and the smelly fleece one beneath. The baby was tiny, smaller than she'd expected, and Liz pushed aside the stab of grief and fear she felt on seeing the fragile, exposed skin red from hypothermia. As the nurse lifted the baby to whisk away the blankets, Liz cut away the footie pajamas and then pulled off the diaper, revealing the gender.

A little girl.

Gauging the heat from the lamp, she pulled it

slightly closer, warming the air around the table a bit more.

With a glance at her watch, she called out, "Someone call for a neonate team to attend, stat." In a quieter voice she continued, "Umbilical stump still attached, inexpertly tied off and cut. I estimate her to be about two days old."

Immediately on placing the baby on the table, Cort had fit his stethoscope into his ears and, as soon as practicable, put it to the tiny chest. Even with that in place, he also pressed fingers into the space between the head and shoulder for good measure, hoping for even the faintest pulse.

One of the nurses fit the oxygen hood over the infant's head, another stood by with electrodes, which Liz took from her and applied. Cort had to shift the chest piece of his scope to allow her to put the second one in place but, even as they were connected, and the agonizing sound of the flatline filled the room, he didn't move from his watch. Liz checked the time.

Thirty seconds.

She knew they had to wait at least a minute before declaring the baby to be without a heartbeat, but the urge to begin CPR was almost overwhelming.

Steady. Steady.

"Forty-five seconds," she said, her voice and the drone of the cardiac monitor the only sounds audible. For a moment it felt as though no one moved, as if even her own breathing had stopped in sympathy. All were caught in the gray area between despair and hope, anticipation of what would come next filling the emergency room with swiftly ratcheting tension.

Then the monitor beeped, just as Cort said, "We have a heartbeat," and they were all in motion again.

"IV," Liz said, putting out her hand. It was difficult to find a vein but she got the needle in place just as the neonate team arrived. Cort stepped back to give them room, stood there as Liz brought them up to speed and they transferred the tiny figure to the rolling incubator in preparation for taking her to the NICU.

With a final flurry they were gone, and Liz exhaled, slowly pulling off her gloves. Cort turned and left the room, and she hurried to catch up to him, cursing under her breath. Just outside the door the police officers stood, one on either side of the door, as if on guard.

"Doc, what's—?"

But Cort, who'd never shown himself to be anything other than courteous and considerate, strode past the cop who was trying to speak to him, as though unaware of the officer's existence. It was left to Liz to stop, and she bit back a surge of annoyance as Cort disappeared down the corridor.

The look on the officer's face stirred her pity, made her think that because of Cort's behavior he expected to hear the worst.

"Officer…"

"Wachowski," he supplied.

"Officer Wachowski, the baby is still alive, though in critical condition, but I'm personally hopeful she'll survive."

He turned away, but not before she saw his face crumple and she knew it was relief making this huge, grizzled officer lose control and cry.

With a hand on his shoulder, she leaned closer, so only he could hear, and said, "You saved that baby's life today. Anything we could do would be useless if it weren't for you. Never forget that, okay?"

He nodded, gulped once, and his voice was

rough and barely audible as he said, "Thanks, Doc."

"It's a girl, Wach," she heard the other officer say, as she took off down the corridor, chased by the sound of back-slapping and relieved laughter. "We need to get some cigars."

Although she searched for him, there was no sign of Cort so, still fuming, Liz went back to work. No doubt he'd avoided her and then gone home, his shift over for the day.

Three hours later, when her shift too came to a close, Liz changed into her street clothes and, unable to resist, made her way up to the sixth-floor neonatal unit.

She'd always been superstitious about certain things, including checking on patients after they'd left the ER and been admitted. More than once another doctor or a nurse had said, "Why didn't you just call for an update, instead of coming all this way?" but that didn't feel right. If she wanted to know how a patient was doing she either checked the system, knowing it might not be up to date, or physically went to check on them. Having not been able to get the tiny baby off her mind, she definitely had to go up and look in on her.

And there, in the NICU, was Cort.

Liz came to a halt, watching through the glass as, the infant held securely in the crook of his arm, he used his foot to move the rocking chair back and forth. Completely focused on the little girl, he was looking down into her face, and the infant seemed to be just as focused on him, her eyes open, unwavering.

His lips moved and, although she couldn't hear him, Liz knew he said, "I've got you, sweetheart. I've got you."

Taking a shaky breath, feeling exposed, stripped bare, Liz backed away, not wanting him to see her; afraid of what was written on her face.

Afraid of the shocking desire rushing through her veins to go in there and hold them both.

CHAPTER FIVE

"JUST CHECKING IN with you." Robbie's voice, annoyingly cheerful, boomed through the phone into her ear. Liz could hear a babble of conversation and peals of laughter behind him. It was early afternoon in London, but it sounded as though a party was already in full swing. "You remember the luncheon, right?"

"Yes. I'm on my way there now."

Not quite accurate, since she'd mislaid her invitation and was actually on her way to the hospital, hoping it was in her locker. While looking for things in her handbag, she had a tendency to pull out whatever was in her way, leaving them where they lay. She'd searched her entire house without finding it, and was trying to convince herself it must be in her work locker. If it wasn't, she was in trouble, since the organizer had specifically said the invitations were necessary for admission.

"Well, have a good time."

Laughter was clear in Robbie's voice. The brat knew how much she hated these types of events.

"Yeah. Sure."

He snickered, then said, "While we're on the subject of favors, I have another one to ask."

"Really? This isn't enough for you?" she teased. "You want to impose on me further, after making me have to spend the morning at the hairdresser and get dressed up?"

"Oh, you're not wearing your scrubs? I'm shocked!"

The over-the-top horror of her brother's comment made her give a snort of laughter.

"That's right, go ahead and make fun of me, even though you want something. See how far that gets you."

When Robbie replied, he'd grown serious. "I want you to be my best woman."

"Your what?"

"Um, best girl? I don't know what to call it. Female best man? Damn it, I want you to stand up with me at my wedding."

Shocked, she said the first thing that came to mind. "But…what about Simon? Didn't you already ask him to be your best man?"

"We've known each other so long he knows

how I feel about you, and he won't mind. Besides, he's already stressing about being in charge of the rings. You know how he is."

She did indeed, since Robbie and Simon had been friends from grade school. "He is a little scatterbrained," she remarked, grimacing at saying so when on her way to try to find her lost invitation.

Misplaced, not lost. Just misplaced.

"And," her brother said quickly, as though sensing he was winning, "I'm a groomsman short, so it would be perfect."

She wasn't surprised to hear that, really. Although Robbie knew lots of people, and had the kind of personality that attracted others to him, when it came to true friends he was highly selective. Liz and he were very different in many ways, but identical in that one.

"Robbie, I don't think—"

Robbie interrupted to say, "Giovanna has already picked out a dress for you to wear and everything."

Liz suppressed a groan. Her mother had sent pictures of not only the wedding dress but the bridesmaids' dress too. They were beautiful. Artistically sublime.

And she would look like hell in one, with far too many curves to do justice to a dress like that.

She was scrambling to figure out the best way to get out of it without hurting her beloved brother's feelings when there was a muffled conversation on the other end of the phone, and then Giovanna came on the line.

"Liz, you must do this. It would mean the world to us. I understood when you said you didn't want to be a bridesmaid, really I did, but this is Robbie asking, not me."

"Giovanna—"

"Liz, we *love* you. It wouldn't be the same if you're not involved."

There was the sensation of being run over by a steamroller, and Liz chuckled, knowing her mother had definitely met her match in her future daughter-in-law.

"I could just wear a morning suit, I guess. To match the men."

"Are you *nuts*?" The outrage was almost palpable. "Not on my watch. Never. But there's a designer in New York who does menswear-inspired formal gowns, and I know I can get her to kit you out. I'll send you a link to her website. When she's done with you, you'll outshine me, with your glorious figure and perfect shoulders."

Liz snorted. "Yeah, sure, Giovanna."

"Trust me, okay? It'll be perfect."

"All right, all right. I see I have one more person in my life I'm not going to be able to say no to. I'll do it. For you. And Robbie."

"Yes!"

Luckily she liked Giovanna too much to be put out by that triumphant crow.

The town car was pulling into the hospital parking lot so she said, "I've got to run. Love to you both, and keep Robbie out of trouble, okay?"

After hanging up, she directed the driver to the staff entrance and, once he'd pulled up, she didn't wait for him to come around and open her door but jumped out.

"I shouldn't be long," she leaned in to say as she pulled her badge out of her handbag. "If they come by and tell you to move, just drive around and meet me back here, please."

Thank goodness the maintenance people had been out and the path to the door had been shoveled and salted. Winter was behaving like a petulant child who was overtired and fighting sleep.

Every time she thought it might be dozing off, it awoke again and had a snow-and-ice tantrum.

Cursing the high-heeled boots she was wearing, Liz held her coat closed and made her way as briskly as possible into the building, then set out at a trot for the changing area. She barreled through the door just in time to be treated to the sight of Cort Smith pulling off a bloodstained scrub top.

It brought her to a screeching halt.

There was the long, strong back she remembered all too well, muscles flexing and rippling the way they had under her grasping, greedy hands. His scrubs bottom hung low on his hips and clung to his perfectly shaped backside. As she stood, frozen in place, watching him, he stretched and yawned, then twisted his head from side to side, as though working out muscle kinks.

She had a few kinks she wouldn't mind having him work out, she thought through the lust fogging her brain.

He reached into his locker for a clean shirt, thankfully still turned away so he wouldn't see her gawping. She tried to get her feet to move, even as her gaze devoured the sheer gorgeousness of him.

The door clicked shut behind her and he looked over his shoulder. For one long moment, which seemed set to stretch into infinity, their gazes locked, and an electric current filled the room, making all the hair on her body rise in a prickling wave.

Mortified to be caught staring, as aroused as all get-out, she sprang into action, aware of her racing heart and the incredible heat rampaging through her body. Willfully keeping her face averted from him, she made it to her locker without falling, although her legs were trembling.

"Hey," he said from behind her. "I thought you were off today."

"I am." Her voice sounded strained, even to her, so she swallowed before she continued. "Just stopped by to try and find an invitation I've mislaid."

"You look...spiffy."

She snorted as she got the locker open and stared at the mess of papers and detritus on the shelf, frustrated at herself for letting it get so bad. "Spiffy? Who on earth uses a word like spiffy? Besides geriatrics and a few nerdy history buffs."

"I do," he said. "Are you calling me old? Because I sucked at history in school."

Her heart was still beating too fast, but the banter, so unexpectedly easy, helped to calm her overexcited system. "If the shoe fits…"

"Really?" Outrage and disgruntlement battled for supremacy in his tone. "It's a perfectly viable word. Perfectly politically correct. Better than saying something inappropriate to your co-worker."

"Inappropriate? Like what?" she asked, glancing at him for an instant over her shoulder. His hair was adorably rumpled from pulling the shirt on over his head, and her fingers tingled with the urge to smooth it, or mess it up even more.

"Like saying she looks delicious enough to eat."

And there went her heart rate again.

Unable to come up with a suitable reply, she desperately shuffled through the teetering stack of bills, notes and other detritus. Where the heck was the darn invitation? He was standing close enough that the subtle scent of him, warm and delicious, wafted over her, all but making her mouth water.

"Where you off to anyway, looking so *spiffy*?"

Normally she wouldn't answer such an intrusive question, but she was still flustered and the words just popped out.

"A luncheon for donors and trustees of philanthropic trusts to meet and network with each other. There's a trust my family administers, and normally my brother would have gone but he's in London with his fiancée for Fashion Week, so it's all on me this time."

"Okay…" It was said slowly, almost hesitantly. "Sounds good."

"Boring as hell," she replied, trying to get back onto the brisk, no-nonsense footing she was used to. "All investment potential, capital growth, and talking about 'beneficial partnerships,' none of which interest me in the slightest. To be honest, I'd rather be lancing a boil than facing this do."

He chuckled, and it seeped into her bones, made her fingers suddenly clumsy, so she pulled too hard on the stack of papers she was riffling through, causing a mini-avalanche. "Dammit."

"So the medical mission to Mexico the HR guy mentioned was arranged by this family trust of yours?"

He sounded merely curious, but the mention

of Mexico brought a fresh wave of heat washing through her.

She'd tried so hard not to think about what had happened on that trip, hoping the after-effects would fade, but now had to admit to herself they hadn't, and probably wouldn't. Perhaps talking about it with Cort would help take the edge off her obsession with it.

And him.

Taking a steadying breath, she turned to face him.

"No. Mexico is outside the trust's purview. It was set up to help organizations here in New York City, where my grand-aunts lived. Do you remember the group of women I was with in Mexico?"

He nodded, a little smile coming and going across those beautifully shaped lips.

"Vaguely."

"We've all been friends from when we were teenagers and don't get that much of a chance to see each other. About six years ago we decided we'd take trips together but make them useful, not just fun. So we take turns picking a place, usually somewhere that has some meaning to us, and the first part of the trip is spent working with locals to do whatever will be of the most help to them. Then we spend the last few days at a resort, relaxing and enjoying ourselves."

His eyebrows quirked upward slightly, and he asked, "You're all doctors?"

Liz chuckled. She couldn't help it, thinking of her friend Jojo, who fainted if she got a paper cut. "No. I'm the only one, so I helped out at the local pediatric clinic while the others did some building repairs and teaching."

"Ah, a pediatric clinic. Does that explain the aqua hair?"

She'd forgotten about the colorful extensions she'd gotten on a whim for the trip, thinking it would be something fun for the kids. It felt strange to think he'd already gotten to know her so well he was able to figure that out.

"It was an icebreaker," she admitted.

His eyelids drooped, concealing whatever thoughts might be given away in his gaze.

"I liked it," he said.

A simple statement, but for some reason it packed a punch. Perhaps it was his expression, which took her right back to that gloriously decadent night they'd shared, or the way his voice dropped low. Whatever the reason, memories bombarded her—of his fingers fisted in her hair, his lips ravaging her throat, the ecstasy building and building until, at his growled demand, she'd imploded.

Insides thrumming with rising want, Liz knew she'd been right not to want to talk about Mexico with him, but it was too late. The remnants of the night swirled between them, creating a sultry current, as warm and humid as the air on the Mayan Riviera. She knew Cort felt it too. He'd gone still, his face tightening to a mask of naked yearning.

Liz shivered, trapped by his desire, and her own. In Mexico, in his arms, she'd felt more a woman than ever before in her life. And now, seeing him once more focused completely, intently on her, the same sensation flowered into being again.

The urge to take the steps necessary to embrace him, pull his head down and kiss him, was so strong Liz wasn't sure how she resisted.

Then, just as suddenly as the expression of desire had appeared on his face, it was gone.

Shaken, Liz tore her gaze away, turning back to her locker. Her hands were trembling, her insides churned with need. She had to get out of there. Now.

Where on earth is that damned invitation?

Cort took a deep breath, but it did nothing to quell his libido. And it definitely needed to be quelled. Liz Prudhomme attracted him in a primal way but, even if he weren't determined to stay away from entanglements of any kind, she'd already run out on him once. No doubt she'd do it again, should he give her a chance. Besides he knew, without a doubt, she was way out of his league socially.

She spoke about philanthropic trusts and London Fashion Week as though they were everyday things that everyday people like him would know all about. Even the way she looked today screamed wealth of the highest order.

In complete contrast to her usual ponytail or simple bob, her hair was upswept in an intricate yet subtly sexy style. And even he, who knew absolutely nothing about designer clothing, could tell there was something special about the long, luxurious-looking coat and knee-high boots she was wearing. The coat fit perfectly over her curves and swung with casual elegance as she moved. Beneath it he glimpsed a teal dress that again, to his eye, looked to have been made just for her.

Liz was all class, and nothing but trouble, and he was kicking himself for wanting her so badly.

She'd gone back to searching her locker, and it felt like a subtle dismissal, yet not even that dulled his desire, or made him leave, the way he knew he should.

What had happened in Mexico hung between them. He couldn't help thinking they would never have a truly easy working relationship until they had talked it out. Clearly the attraction between them hadn't abated, and he wasn't sure what that would mean. All he knew was that he was compelled to let her know where he stood, no matter where it eventually led.

"I know you don't want to talk about Mexico."

"You're right," she replied briskly, as another little cascade of papers fell from her locker. "So let's not."

"Too late," he retorted, and saw her shoulders stiffen slightly. "Listen, we're both adults, and it's best we deal with what happened between us. It was an amazing night. One I'll never forget. I was angry, and lonely, and you helped me forget the pain and embarrassment, even if just for one night. But, although I'm still extremely attracted to you, I'm not going to try to get back into your bed, because..."

Why not?

He took a breath, considering what he needed to say next. Liz's fingers stilled, her hunt paused as she waited for him to continue. His brain scrambled for the reasons, knowing they were many, trying to move past the attraction and get to the reality.

"Not only do we work together, but I don't want to lead you on. I've come to realize I'm not cut out for long-term relationships. Couldn't offer you anything more than the chance to keep scratching the itch, the way we did in Mexico."

She looked at him over her shoulder, eyebrows raised, her gaze searching his. "But you were about to get married. I'd think that would have been a long-term relationship, don't you?"

He nodded. "Sure, but I realized having the wedding called off was a good thing. There were...extenuating circumstances that caused me to sort of drift into a situation I really shouldn't have."

"How does one drift into an engagement?" she asked, not derisively but obviously curious.

His first urge was to deflect the question, but something about the way she looked at him drew the words from his lips.

"Mimi, my ex, was there for me during a bad time in my life, and gave me the support I needed. It was only after she ended our relationship that I realized we'd mistaken our friendship for something more than it was."

Her eyes narrowed slightly, but her gaze was level as she said, "When we met, you were pretty upset about the break-up. How can you be so casual about it now?"

Cort sighed. He must sound like the kind of guy who shrugged things off when he didn't get what he wanted, and somehow the thought of her pegging him like that was abhorrent.

"I've had some time to think it through, to realize that, while her rejection hurt like hell, we really wouldn't have been happy together. I have itchy feet, Liz. Being in the army alleviated some of that, even though the coveted posting to Hawaii never materialized."

That made the corners of her lips twitch, but when she didn't say anything he continued. "I stayed in Denver too long, and now I'm determined not to settle in any one place for any length of time again. I've never spent any time in New York, and there's a lot to explore, but once my contract is up next year, I'll more than likely move on."

Liz seemed to be considering what he'd said, her gaze searching his face. He'd come to realize she was a thinker, one of those people who liked to mull things over and rarely acted impulsively. It was obvious in how she handled patients and their families, as well as the people she worked with, although in an emergency she was absolutely decisive.

So it came as no surprise when she just made a noncommittal sound in the back of her throat before diving back into her locker.

Taking that as a clear dismissal, he was about to leave then remembered there was something more he wanted to tell her.

"On a totally different subject, I thought you'd want to know. The police cleared Kaitlin of wrongdoing. From the forensic evidence, she shot her boyfriend in self-defense."

"Good to know," she replied, emerging triumphantly with an embossed card in her hand.

When she bent to pick up the bits of paper that had spilled out onto the floor, he stooped to help her and was surprised by the obvious anger in her expression.

"You're angry that it was self-defense?"

"What? No! Why would you ask such a question?"

"Oh, maybe the way your brows are scrunched together, the slight snarl on your lips."

Cort thought that would, at least, merit a snort or the Liz Prudhomme version of a smile, which consisted of a twitch of the lips, but her frown just deepened.

"He beat and stabbed her, almost to death, and all she was worried about was that she'd shot him to save herself. Even when I went to ICU to see her, she was asking about him. I don't get it. I really don't."

Getting up, she shoved the papers back into her locker and slammed the door. Cort shook his head. He didn't get it either, but he'd seen it too many times not to know the answer. "She'd say she loves him."

Liz snorted then, but not with anything close to amusement, as she picked up her handbag and headed for the door. "Makes no sense to me.

Never has. Never will. That's not love. That's some kind of terminal disease that weakens the brain."

Yanking the door open, she turned back and said, "Wait, that sounds like an accurate definition, doesn't it? At least, from everything *I've* seen."

Then she was gone, leaving Cort stunned at the emotion in her voice, which had turned the decadent tones into something rougher. Raw.

It was not the kind of response he expected from the no-nonsense Dr. Liz Prudhomme.

CHAPTER SIX

Dr. Hammond's secretary looked up as Cort opened the door and, without pausing in her telephone conversation, jerked her head toward the inner office. Taking the gesture from the stern, gray-haired lady as an indication he should continue straight through, Cort thanked her with a wave. He knocked on Gregory's door and, when the chief of surgery called out, entered the sunny, cluttered office.

"There you are." The smile on Gregory's face had the tension in Cort's shoulders easing fractionally. "And right on time too. Come. Sit."

Making his way to the stiffly stuffed chair across the desk from his boss, Cort did as bade, still unsure about the reason for the summons. There was no way to get comfortable in the visitor's seat, probably by design, but he forced himself not to search for one. Instead, he simply propped one ankle up on the opposite knee and resigned himself to the ache he'd no doubt develop in his back if the interview went on too long.

He also figured it best to cut right to the chase.

"Is there a problem, Gregory?"

"No, not at all." The older man leaned back, linking his fingers behind his neck, the picture of ease. "I thought, since you've been with us for a little over a month now, it was time to check in with you and see how you're getting along."

That was surprising. Cort had been almost completely sure Liz had complained about his takeover of the infant emergency case, had been prepared to apologize and reassure everyone it would never happen again. Even though that really wasn't a promise he could truthfully make.

"Everything is fine so far." There really was nothing he could complain about to Gregory. All his issues with being at the hospital revolved around one strong, sexy doctor, who was never far from his thoughts.

"Glad to hear it." Gregory rocked back and forth. "I know things are a bit slower than you're used to in the trauma department, but the board has said the construction should be finished in another few months. Things will definitely pick up soon thereafter."

"I'm sure they will," he agreed.

"And how are things otherwise? Did you get your house in Denver sold, and have you found something appropriate here?"

"Finally got an offer on the house last week, and hopefully it'll close in thirty days," Cort replied, giving the older man a rueful smile. "But as for here? To be honest, I haven't really been looking very hard."

He didn't feel the need to house-hunt. He'd only bought the house in Denver because he and Mimi had been getting married and it had seemed appropriate. His New York apartment, while small, was perfectly suitable for the year. Of course, he wasn't planning to say that to Dr. Hammond, who no doubt hoped Cort would be a permanent member of his surgical team.

Gregory shook his head, and sat forward with a thump of feet hitting the floor. "No, no, Cort. If you want to stay anywhere within the vicinity of the hospital, with the gentrification now is the time to buy. Even if you eventually leave Hepplewhite General, and I hope that won't be for many years, by then the property should have appreciated nicely." The telephone on his desk buzzed, and Gregory put his hand on it but didn't pick it up right away. "Well, unless there's anything you want to discuss..."

Cort levered himself from the chair. "No, thank you, Gregory."

"Excellent." Gregory smiled, but he was already looking at his phone, and Cort strode to the door and let himself out, just as he heard the other man say, "Yes, Brenda?"

Brenda, the secretary, was speaking in a discreetly low tone into the phone when Cort walked through her office and didn't look up from her computer screen, so missed his goodbye wave.

That annoyed him a little. No matter what your position in life, there was no need to be ill-mannered. No doubt, as Gregory's secretary, she had to be firm with some of the doctors, perhaps even patients too, but there were ways to do that without being rude.

Like the way Liz handled things, straight up but never impolite.

He mentally kicked himself for thinking about her again, yet she continually invaded his consciousness like a super-bug, impervious to every course of treatment he came up with to oust her.

As he'd told her the day before, there were at least two really good reasons for them not to be together again, but unfortunately neither stopped him wanting her. The way she'd run out on him in Mexico still stung too, especially now he'd gotten to know her day-to-day persona better. Had that night never happened, he'd have sworn Liz Prudhomme wasn't the kind of woman who'd sneak away without saying a word or even leaving a note. She was too no-nonsense and polite, too straightforward. The anomaly of what he thought of her and the reality of that night should be a warning and have tempered the longing, but hadn't.

There was something about her that called to him and that draw of hers was a source of constant distraction and annoyance.

He forewent the elevator, opting for the stairs, hoping to work off some of his frustration.

Avoiding entanglements was the right thing to do, he reminded himself as he pounded down the stairs. Getting too involved with people just caused pain, and he was tired of being hurt.

So many good reasons to avoid Liz and squelch the attraction still dogging him. In time to the slap of his feet on the steps, he listed them in his head one more time, hoping they'd finally take root in his stubborn brain.

She was a colleague, and he had to work with her almost every day.

He had a life plan all worked out, which didn't include sticking around in New York City for very long. There were new places to discover, new worlds to explore, and he who travelled fastest travelled alone.

Best of all, he already had proof she was the kind of woman who had no compunction about leaving a person high and dry, without explanation.

Like his parents had, when they'd abandoned him as a baby.

Like Brody had, without giving Cort a chance to help him through his pain.

Pushing open the door to the on-call room, he was glad to see there was no one there. Letting out a relieved sigh, he moved to the coffee station and poured himself a cup. Thankfully the meeting with Gregory hadn't taken as long as he'd thought it would, so he had time to gather his thoughts before his shift started.

He'd been sure there would have been a complaint regarding his conduct when Baby Jane, as the unidentified infant was being called, had come in. Even now, the memory of hearing the nurse call out about the baby being found in a dumpster raised goose bumps down his spine.

It was like being present at his own finding, the instinct to help another foundling so strong it had completely blocked all thoughts of protocol.

Why hadn't Liz complained? He'd been certain that she would.

The woman was a mass of contradictions.

Some of the nurses called her "Dr. Grim," yet it was said with a certain amused fondness that told him they actually liked her. Many of the doctors grumbled about her stoic demeanor, but not one touted her as being anything but a superb practitioner. Everyone knew she was a stickler for protocol, and it was clear Cort had overstepped his bounds by a mile. Not reporting him to Hammond was totally out of character for her.

And he didn't like it that he was beginning to know her so well.

Getting to understand her on a personal level wouldn't help him at all. Easier to get past his attraction if he could keep his interest in her purely professional. He had no interest in getting close to Liz Prudhomme in any way other than they already had been.

Carnally, erotically, sexually.

He drew in a sharp breath at the memory of her arching beneath his caresses, shuddering with release. Trying to push aside the images just made them somehow sharper, and it was as though he could feel her legs around his waist again, the slick pulses of her body gripping his, the swift, sweet ache of her biting his shoulder as she'd come.

Taking a too-hot gulp of coffee, he cursed. Yet he welcomed the burn of tongue and throat. It forced some modicum of control, allowing him the opportunity to settle his breathing and will away the unwanted erection pushing at the front of his scrubs.

That was in the past, never to happen again, he forcefully reminded himself. The sooner he took that fully on board, and stopped obsessing over one night in Mexico, the better it would be for his peace of mind.

The door behind him opened and he turned, a polite expression firmly in place, to see who it was.

And, just like that, he had to marshal his willpower all over again as he stared into Liz's gleaming green eyes.

He would have greeted her, but something

about her expression kept him frozen in watchful silence. She was leaning on the door, as though to stop anyone else from entering, both palms pressed against the wood, fingers slightly curled, and something about the position of her hands stirred that ever-present desire again.

The silence seemed to stretch on forever as she looked around the room before she quietly said, "I want you to know, I'm not interested in a relationship."

Surprise was too mild a word for what he felt, and a harsh bark of laughter came from his throat. Her eyebrows dipped together as he replied, "I told you, I'm not either."

"But I want you, physically. If you're interested, can you deal with that? Sex without any kind of commitment?"

His heart was pounding, and his impulse was to agree quickly, before she changed her mind, but he turned what she said over in his mind first, strangely prudent in the face of what looked like her impulsiveness.

"I can do that," he said slowly, inwardly cursing himself for what he was going to say next. Knowing it would probably make her change her mind. "But you should know, I actually *like* you. What happens if we become friends?"

She tilted her head slightly, as though this was an eventuality she hadn't considered, her gaze searching his intently. Whatever she saw there seemed to satisfy her because she nodded and asked, "Do you know where the old isolation ward is?"

"Yes." Gregory Hammond had shown it to him on the first day, while they'd toured the construction zone. Cort was pretty sure he remembered how to get to it.

"Meet me there in five minutes."

Then, without another word, she spun on her heel and pulled open the door.

It wasn't until the door closed completely that Cort could exhale, and there definitely was nothing he could do about the need tearing through his system.

Slapping his coffee cup down onto the table, he glanced at his watch.

He was sure it would be the longest five minutes of his life.

If Liz knew one thing about herself it was that she tried to face things head on and didn't back away from the truth, even if she was the only one who knew what that truth was. That facet of her personality made her come to accept the fact she had to do something about Dr. Cort Smith, something to exorcise the hold he had on her imagination and libido.

He'd taken over her mind in a way she'd never experienced before, filling her with yearnings she didn't know how to control.

It was, she told herself, simply that he'd given her the most memorable night of sex she'd ever had, and then, to add insult to injury, had touched her emotionally too. Seeing him so tenderly holding the baby in the NICU had been like having the wall around the feelings she so fiercely guarded severely dented.

On the one hand, she hated him for it. On the other, it made her want him ten times, a hundred times more than she already did. The conversation in the changing room had just cemented the longing that had shimmered beneath her skin from the first night they'd met.

Striding down the corridor past the heavy plastic sheeting, from beyond which came the noise of the construction workers, she once more reassured herself she was taking the right course in dealing with Cort.

He had taken her to new heights with his dominant style in bed, giving her more pleasure than she'd even suspected was possible. A shiver worked its way along her spine and heat blossomed low in her belly as she remembered it once again. That pleasure that had lingered in her system, rather like a bad case of the flu or Lyme disease, she thought rather sourly. She needed an antidote, and perhaps familiarity would provide it.

After all, their encounter in Mexico had happened before he'd known her, before he'd seen her at work or worked alongside her.

Now he'd had a chance to see her the way others had and did. To her family, and to Andrew, she was a tough, cool, unemotional woman, used to taking charge, unwilling to relinquish her control.

Would he still feel comfortable taking command of her body the way he had before?

She doubted it. And if he didn't, she was quite sure she'd lose interest in him very, very quickly.

And if he did, then at least she'd have the chance at the physical satisfaction she craved.

His stated aversion to a relationship made it all the better. Unlike Andrew, Cort at least was honest about that, and about his wanderlust. She could go into this knowing there wouldn't be complications. That she wouldn't be blindsided by unreasonable expectations or a sudden abandonment when those expectations weren't met.

Reaching the end of the corridor and leaving the main construction zone behind, she turned down another hallway, then made a quick left into the isolation ward. It had been packed with some of the equipment they'd had to store during the expansion, so that on entering the room she was presented with what looked a bit like a maze. And, as she stood a couple of steps from the door, she was suddenly assailed with something akin to fear. It held her where she was, her back toward the door, heart pounding, lust like quicksilver in her veins. Her legs trembled as the need in her core spread outwards and her nipples ached in anticipation.

Not fear, she reassured herself. Desire, and the overwhelming need to know whether Cort would assuage it or be found lacking this time around.

She wasn't sure which she'd prefer...

The quiet click of the door opening had her

scrambling for enough control to turn and face him, but she didn't get a chance to pull herself together before his deep voice reached her.

"Are we here to talk, or something else?" He was close behind her. The heat pouring off his body made gooseflesh pop up all along her back and arms, and had her breath catching in her throat. "I'm taking nothing for granted when it comes to you, Liz, so tell me why I'm here."

"I want you." The words flowed far too easily from her lips, but it was the truth, and she was big on the truth, even if she didn't feel ready to face him just yet. "Right now."

"Good." It was a growl, and he surrounded her with his strong, solid arms, the hardness of his erection pressing between her buttocks. "I wasn't sure I'd be able to restrain myself if you wanted a discussion."

She would have replied, except he nipped her nape, the sharp scrape of his teeth along the sensitive skin making her breath hitch and her mind stumble over its thoughts.

"Over here," he said, the harshness of his voice striking sparks over her skin, ratcheting up the tension in her core. He curved his arms tighter around her waist and half guided, half carried her between two fabric-shrouded machines into the dim space beyond. She caught a quick glance of more machinery, some gurneys, other unidentifiable shapes, before he turned her within his arms and kissed her.

Her bones went liquid. The rush of lust engendered just by the touch of his lips on hers, the tangle of their tongues was almost too much to bear. A moan rose in her throat and she couldn't curtail it. The sound, needy and rushed, was one she couldn't recall ever hearing herself make before. When she felt the cool of a wall against her back, she arched into Cort, her need all she was aware of.

Strong hands tugged her scrub top up, and she raised her arms, eager for it to be gone, to get flesh-to-flesh with Cort. They broke the kiss to be able to get it off, but when Liz turned her face, searching for his lips, and wound her arms around his neck again, Cort didn't respond the way she expected. Instead of kissing her again, he dropped her top and grasped her wrists, lifting them above her head and holding them there with one hand.

"You've made me crazy." His free hand slid down her arm to skim the side of her breast through the remainder of her clothing. Just that indirect touch made her tremble, yearn. "You owe me."

"For what?" She had to force the words out past the desperation clogging her throat.

The sound he made was possibly supposed to have been a chuckle, but it came out as a snarl. "For every swing of your hips as you walked down the corridors. For every word you've spoken to me since I got here. For every look from those beautiful eyes." He let his voice trail away, his dark gaze holding hers effortlessly in the gloom as his fingers found her nipple, pinched, and proved he remembered exactly what turned her on. "I want payment."

"With what?"

She tried to make her voice defiant, amused, but there was no mistaking the slight tremor in the words. Cort smiled, a predatory, knowing grin she could see even in the low light. When he leaned in and put his lips close to her ear, Liz already knew she was in trouble before he whispered, "Your pleasure. And mine."

When had he lifted the camisole she wore under her scrubs? And how had he got her bra undone with one hand? Then the questions were driven from her mind by the sensation of his mouth on her breasts, the promise made by his pushing her scrub bottoms and panties down to her knees.

Desperation rose in her, she was already so close to the edge. The urge to widen her stance, give him full access, made her shift her legs, restlessly trying to work her pants down farther. He said, "Stay still."

With arms still upraised, although he'd let them go, Liz froze, shivering at the command in his tone, at the way her desire flared even higher. It was like Mexico all over again, when he'd held her in thrall, taken her compliance and turned it into ecstasy. As he kissed and nipped and sucked his way down her body, it felt as if time slowed, warped, and it took forever for him to reach where she wanted him; where she needed him to touch. When she finally felt the heat of his breath between her thighs, she again wanted to open for him, but his injunction to remain still held her where she was.

"Don't hold back," he said, the words vibrating into her flesh, making her bite her lip to stop from begging, her breathing so erratic she felt light-headed. "Come for me, Liz. Come hard."

And when he pressed his mouth against her, it took only the lightest touch for her to explode.

"Good girl," he groaned against her still-quivering flesh. "And one more…"

CHAPTER SEVEN

Liz made a quick dash into the ladies' room, which was thankfully empty.

Her legs were trembling, her body humming with endorphins. As she washed her hands and splashed cold water on her face, she tried to put aside all thought of what had just transpired. According to the page she'd just got, there were casualties coming in from a multivehicle accident so she needed to be prepared, not shaky and discombobulated.

She'd think about the fact Cort Smith had once more rocked her world later. Much later.

After all, it was just sex.

Fabulous sex.

But just sex.

Nothing worth disrupting her life over.

If nothing else, she had her answer. Getting him out of her system would probably be more difficult than she had anticipated. Yet they had an agreement. No entanglements, no repercussions from their pleasure. No bleeding over from the personal into the professional. And she would swiftly put an end to this new arrangement if he made the mistake of changing the way he behaved toward her on the hospital floor.

She'd been brutally honest about not being interested in a relationship, and he'd said the same. Hopefully she really could trust him to stand by their agreement to not get in any way attached. It wasn't that she thought herself irresistible or anything like that, just that men hardly ever said what they meant or stood by their agreements. She'd be on guard for any change in his behavior, and that was the best she could do. She was still sure that propositioning him again had been the right idea, even though something niggled at the back of her mind, trying to sow doubt.

Perhaps it was how much his personality reminded her of Andrew. The charm that had people falling over themselves to please him, and had them gravitating into his sphere. She'd fallen for that once and refused to fall for it again. Men like him would suck you dry, demanding you change to suit them better, and then, when you were willing to do anything to keep them, left you anyway. At least Cort had been up front in saying he wouldn't be around for very long, and Liz had no intention of allowing herself to get emotionally involved in any way.

What he'd said about them becoming friends didn't deserve a lot of consideration. She'd never made friends easily and guarded her friendships fiercely. Her friends could be counted on the fingers of one hand and were people who accepted her as she was, without expectation that she'd change to suit them or the situation. Who understood that to ask her opinion was to get an honest answer, even if she knew it wasn't what they wanted to hear. Perhaps her only male friend was Robbie, and did he even count as he was her brother too?

There was a lot to think about now that she'd taken this irrevocable step, but she'd never been the type to dwell, or have regrets, or constantly rehash every decision she made, and she wasn't going to start now.

Giving herself a last long look in the mirror, hoping no one would notice how puffy her lips were, she strode out of the restroom, heading for the ER.

By the time the first casualties got to the hospital, Liz and the rest of the staff were braced for the controlled chaos to come. A tour bus, on its way out of the city, had struck a couple of cars and gone off the road. The more severely injured patients were being sent to Roosevelt, the nearest level one center, with the rest of the injured being distributed between Hepplewhite and another level two facility.

She just had time to notice Cort putting on a disposable gown before the first ambulances pulled up. For an instant their gazes locked, and a shiver raced down her spine. Then the doors flew open and the gurneys started coming in, and she had no time to think about anything but her patients.

And it was only at the end of the long, grueling day she realized there'd been no awkwardness. They'd worked together as smoothly as they had since he'd arrived, treating a couple of patients together without even an untoward glance or comment from him. And, although her heart still did that silly dip when she heard his voice, she was pleased to realize the anxiety and desire that had kept her on edge seemed to have waned.

It seemed as though her plan to mitigate her reaction to him might just be working after all.

* * *

Cort couldn't find an ounce of regret about his tryst with Liz, although part of him was kicking himself for letting it happen.

There had been no postmortem between them. No questioning whether it had been right or wrong, good or not as good as either of them remembered. Her beeper had gone off and, with calm deliberation, she'd righted her clothes and given him one of her clear-eyed looks.

"I have to run," she said. A ghost of a smile had the corners of her lips twitching momentarily upward. "Although that will be difficult, since I can hardly feel my legs."

Then, just like that, she was gone, leaving him wondering exactly what the backlash of what had just occurred would be.

It was stupid to have given in to his desire for her, he knew. Complicating a working relationship with sex wasn't smart, and never ended well.

And sex was all it was, or could be.

Yet, despite his worries, Liz Prudhomme treated him exactly the same way she had before.

Although it went against his better judgment to have a sexual affair at work, it also made sense to keep it casual, and taking it outside the hospital felt like taking it a step further than either of them wanted.

So, after that first time in the isolation ward, they found other places to be together whenever they could. Liz, Cort came to find out, was completely open when it came to where, when and how he pleasured her and took pleasure in her body. And he became diabolically inventive in finding places and ways to please her. It shocked him a bit. He'd never considered himself the type to have an affair with a workmate, but he couldn't seem to stay away from Liz.

Every encounter just made him want her more, although he was as determined as she'd said she was to keep it purely physical. Occasionally they had the same day off, with the ER and surgical team having different schedules, but there was never a suggestion, from either of them, that they take it outside the hospital.

There was no future for them, so it seemed ridiculous to intertwine their lives more than they already were.

Because of their schedules they were usually able to grab only a half hour or so together, just enough for him to make her crazy with lust and then send them both flying. He sometimes wondered if it was wrong to continue what he knew was a dead-end affair. Yet since Liz didn't seem to mind and, in fact, never indicated any wish for anything more, he let it ride. It felt too good to stop.

No, not good. Amazing.

Something about the way she surrendered to him, gave in to his demands, found obvious satisfaction in what they did together, was surprising, but he loved every minute of it.

So they met wherever they could be assured of a few minutes of privacy. In storage closets, the isolation ward, the construction zone on the weekend when the workers weren't around. Even, on one memorable occasion, in the rest area off the on-call room, when neither of them could bear to wait.

He'd sat on the narrow cot and pulled her to straddle his thighs, and the similarity to the first time they'd been together in Mexico had seemed to echo between them, heightening both their arousals. He'd known she'd been ready but had wanted it to last so, instead of telling her to let go and find her release, he'd told her to wait, kept her on the knife-edge for several long, deep strokes, before commanding her to come. His own orgasm had been so powerful it had been almost painful. Just thinking about it made his head want to explode all over again. Liz had that kind of effect on him every time they were together.

They might have gone on that way forever or, at least, a lot longer, if they hadn't almost got caught in flagrante delicto about a month after they'd started having their trysts around the hospital.

It had been in the old isolation ward, with him behind Liz, buried deep in the sweet, wet heat of her body. The arch of her back and trembling of her legs, the way she'd rhythmically clenched around him as he'd thrust had told him she was close. He'd pinched her nipples the way he knew she loved, hard enough to take her almost over into orgasm, when the door opened and the lights came on, almost blinding him.

Cort froze, of course, suddenly furious with himself, and her. They were deep in the maze of equipment and beds, but he still glanced over his shoulder, hoping they weren't visible from the doorway. Not that that would help them should the people entering the room start walking around.

"Over the next couple of days, we'll start pulling out the equipment that needs to be installed." He recognized the voice of Jennifer Marshalec, the administrator in charge of the expansion, who sounded as though she was coming farther into the room. "I want to take a look around now to see exactly what we have here. The inventory lists I found really don't seem complete to me."

There was a deep murmur in response, and Cort felt a burst of adrenaline fire through his veins. His brain was swirling with five hundred different thoughts. Should they take the chance of being heard and try to re-dress, or stay still? Was there another way out of the room, or somewhere to hide until Jennifer and whoever she was with were gone?

I'm too old to play hide-and-seek...

"Okay, we'll start—" A phone rang. "Excuse me a moment. Hello? Yes. Oh, for goodness' sake, I'm not at my desk..." Jennifer sighed extravagantly. "Okay, give me five minutes. I'll call you back. Ramone, I'll come back down in a little while and we can continue."

"Sure, Ms. Marshalec." Ramone sounded bored. "I'll be in the construction office when you're ready."

Cort heard the tip-tap of Jennifer's heels and the clump of Ramone's boots as they headed for the exit. The light went out, the noises from outside flared and then were once more cut off by the closing of the door.

Neither of them moved right away, but Liz was trembling, her entire body quaking…

With laughter?

"Oh, really?" Cort growled into her ear. "That wasn't funny. Not…at…all."

With each of the last words he stroked into her, long and deep, and, to his shock, realized the fear of discovery had only stoked the flames of his desire. It seemed to have had the same effect on Liz. She pushed back to meet his every thrust until, still shaking with what was apparently laughter, he felt the quickening of her movements and she came apart on his command, just as always.

Afterward, Cort didn't said anything. In fact, he didn't speak to her, other than in a purely professional way, for a couple of days. There was a lot to think about and, still angry at the risks they'd taken, he didn't want to go off half-cocked.

Realistically, he enjoyed what they had very

much, but he wasn't willing to risk his career to keep it up. If she wanted them to keep sleeping together, they'd have to take it outside the hospital. That was, after all his ruminating, the final analysis. Whether she agreed or not was up to her, and he'd abide by her decision.

He rather hoped she was willing to go on seeing him since he was reluctant to see it end.

When he finally brought up the subject, he had no choice, in his own mind, but to give her an ultimatum.

"We can't keep taking chances at the hospital, Liz." He said it dispassionately and when she looked away, instead of meeting his gaze in her usual forthright manner, his chest tightened. It was just as well, really. He didn't want her to guess how much he hoped she'd agree. "I don't want to jeopardize either of our jobs anymore. I think we were a little crazy to be doing this to begin with."

"I understand." Her voice was steady, almost but not quite uninterested.

The tone made his jaw clench, but he decided to ignore it. "So, hereafter, if you want to see me, we're going to have to meet outside work." She shot him a quick glance, her intent, seeking gaze scouring his face. "You can come to my place if you'd like."

For a long moment she didn't say anything, just looked at him, her head to one side. When she finally spoke, he realized he'd been holding his breath the entire time.

"I realize we can't continue the way we've been going, but I still don't want a relationship." She lifted one hand, as though to take back the words, and then let it drop. "Not that what we have isn't a *kind* of relationship, but you know what I mean."

"I'm not asking you for anything you don't want to give, and I think it's safe to say things were going along the way we'd agreed." He kept his voice as matter-of-fact as hers had been, although it took some effort. "I'm just saying I, honestly, don't really want it to stop. I just won't keep it up here. That's all."

She nodded, glanced away again, as though considering what he'd said. It was her way, giving everything deep thought before responding, but knowing that didn't stop his heart from racing or sweat from building along his spine.

It's just sex, he reminded himself. *Don't make*

it more important than it is. But knowing that didn't reduce his stress level.

Finally she nodded again, looked at him with a bland, noncommittal expression. "Okay. We can try it, see how it goes."

Why was he so relieved? Cort took a prescription insert out of his pocket and found a spot to write on. The effort needed to concentrate on what he was doing was a welcome excuse not to keep looking at her, so hopefully she wouldn't see how much it meant that she was at least considering it. When he held the sheet out to her, and she took it, the relief morphed to elation.

"This is my cell number and address. We'll work out the timing when we get a chance."

"Okay," she said, taking the paper from his hand, a hint of some emotion he didn't recognize breaking through her level tone.

Was she annoyed? Fed up? He couldn't tell, but was left with the distinct impression that hearing from her was out of the question. Which was why he was frankly shocked when he got a text from her just as he was preparing to leave the hospital at the end of his shift that same day.

Will you be at home later?

Cort stood, staring at his phone, wondering if it was a figment of his imagination brought on by his driving need for her.

"Everything okay?" Reggie Morrison asked.

"Hmm?" Cort looked over at the other surgeon, who was also getting ready to go home. "I'm sorry. What?"

Reggie slammed his locker door shut. "I asked if everything was okay." He lifted his chin toward the phone still clutched in Cort's hand. "You're glaring at that phone as though you want to strangle it."

"Oh, yeah. Everything's fine." Cort managed a smile and stuck the phone into his pocket. "Just an unexpected message."

"You still meeting us at the Red Rover Inn later?" Having plopped onto the bench, Reggie was putting on his street shoes. "Last I heard we were aiming for seven."

"No." There was no way he would put off Liz just to have drinks with the guys. "I don't think I can make it. Give the others my apologies, would you?"

"Sure." Reggie got up and stretched. "Maybe next time?"

"Definitely." Cort pretended to be engrossed

with something in his locker, desperate for a little privacy. He had a message to answer. "Have a good time."

"Will do." Reggie lifted a hand in farewell. "Bye."

"Bye."

Cort whipped his phone back out even before the locker-room door closed.

CHAPTER EIGHT

OKAY, SO SHE was weak.

Pathetic even.

When Cort had issued his ultimatum she'd walked away, already having decided to tell him to go to hell. Instead, here she was on her way to his place.

Liz switched the bag of Chinese takeout from one hand to the other so she could wipe the sweat off her palms on the legs of her jeans.

It's not a date. More like...um...a tryst. Yeah. A tryst.

Yet thinking that didn't make her feel any less nervous. It had been a very, very long time since she'd gone out of her way to be with a man, other than just for sex. Cort may have said he wanted to continue what had, to that point, been strictly a sexual relationship, but going to his place bearing food from her favorite Chinese restaurant smacked of it becoming something more.

And it was that *more* she'd been assiduously avoiding.

She couldn't help thinking of how Andrew had charmed her into doing whatever he'd wanted, no matter what her instincts had been saying. The resentment she felt now seemed an echo of those times, and she cursed herself for a fool. She should have told him to go to hell.

"Too late now," she muttered to herself, stepping out of the elevator onto the floor where Cort's apartment was. Taking a deep breath, reminding herself she didn't have to stay, or come back if it didn't go the way she wanted, she marched up to his door and rang the bell. It felt as though it took forever for Cort to answer. By the time he did, she'd tried to convince herself to leave one more time, then talked herself out of it again by remembering just how incredible he made her feel.

It's just for sex...

When she heard the sound of the door being unlocked, she stiffened and held her breath.

"Hi." Cort stood there, smiling, and despite her anxiety, or maybe because of it, Liz's heart fluttered. He pulled the door open wider and stepped back, gesturing her inside with a sweep of his hand. "Come on in."

Not sure whether to be annoyed or relieved that he hadn't done something trite like kiss or hug her, Liz took him up on the invitation. Once inside, she pushed back the hood of her jacket and thrust the bag of food toward him. "I got Chinese. Wasn't sure what you'd like, so a got a bunch of different dishes."

Good grief. She was babbling, and forced her lips shut to stop it. The visceral response she experienced whenever she saw Cort was magnified by being in his home, making her brain race and her heart thump.

"I'm sure it'll be fine." Still smiling, he closed the door. "You can hang your coat in the closet there."

Cort disappeared around a corner, into the kitchen, she suspected as she unwound her scarf and opened the door he'd indicated. Unlike her own hall closet, which often looked as though a bomb had gone off in it, his was incredibly neat. She shrugged out of her winter coat and then hung it, together with her scarf, on a free hanger. Then she perched on the bench near the door and took off her boots. With a deep breath, she got up and went after Cort.

He was, indeed, in his galley kitchen, which was separated from a living/dining room by an island, on which he was unpacking the food. He glanced at her and smiled without pausing in what he was doing.

"Have a seat. What'll you have to drink?"

"Just water, thanks." Ignoring his suggestion to sit, she prowled around the room, taking it all in.

The rest of the apartment was as neat as the hall closet but had an unfinished, hardly lived-in feel. Yes, there was a sectional and an easy chair that toned with it, and a small bar-height dining table surrounded by four chairs. Sure, there was a coffee table and an end table, and a large-screen TV, but there was also a lack of decorative touches. No pictures or mementos on the console beneath the TV, no paintings on the walls. Not to mention the pile of boxes in the corner. Not that any of it was her business anyway...

"Not settled in yet?"

She could have bitten off her own tongue for giving in to her urge for small talk. That wasn't why she was here.

"No." He was clattering stuff around in the

kitchen, doing who knew what. "It didn't seem to make sense to unpack, only to have to pack it all up again in a year. Actually, any box that I don't open between now and then I'll probably just throw away."

"Hmm." Restless, not knowing what to do with herself, she moved closer to the boxes. Although handwritten, the labels all looked exactly alike and were aligned on the boxes in precisely the same way. He'd been in the military, she remembered, so maybe that type of precision and his neatness were holdovers from his training. Not a bad trait for a surgeon to possess. "'C. M. Smith,'" she read aloud. Cort wasn't really a name, was it? It must be short for something. "What's your full name anyway?"

Maybe it was the sudden silence, or the fact he didn't answer right away, but whatever it was had Liz turning to look at him. When he glanced up at her, his face was noncommittal, and the expression had her antennae quivering.

"Cortland Main Smith."

"*Maine*, as in the state?" She drew closer to the island as he turned his back to her and opened a drawer.

"Nope, just *M-A-I-N*."

"Cortland Main." Liz sat on one of the bar stools, all her focus on the man setting chopsticks on the counter in front of her. "Interesting names. Are they traditional to your family?"

"No."

The curtness of his reply took her by surprise, but she only said, "I'm not judging, believe me. My full name is Eliza Honoria." That got the expected response of raised eyebrows and a barely controlled upward twitch of his lips. "My parents had the bright idea of naming me after two of my father's old aunts who never married, hoping they would leave him something in their wills."

He was trying manfully not to laugh, but she was sure she still read tension in the set of his shoulders. "Did it work?"

The old bitterness-tinged amusement rose in her. "Nope. At least, not the way my parents wanted it to. My great-aunts were the ones who left the trust I told you about, the one I had to go to that damned luncheon for. But don't change the subject. How did your parents come up with your names?"

"They didn't." Both hands on the counter, he held her gaze. There again was that noncommittal expression, but his eyes were too carefully shielded. "Child protection agents gave me that name after I was found in a cardboard box at the corner of Cortland Road and Main Street."

Cort waited for Liz's reaction, his skin clammy, his heart pounding. There were few people who knew his story and how she reacted would determine where they went from here. He didn't need pity, or to be looked down on because of his rootless existence.

Liz's eyes widened, but he should have known she wouldn't react like anyone else.

"Oh, that explains it," she said, her gaze clear, penetrating. He must have shown some sign of his surprise at her matter-of-fact comment because she added, "Your reaction to Baby Jane coming in. Were you hypothermic too, when they found you?"

"A bit." He watched as she almost unconsciously picked up the chopsticks in front of her and dipped into one of the containers of food. As she popped a piece of Schezuan chicken between her lips, he found himself continuing, "It was early spring, still cold."

"Hmm." She finished chewing, swallowed, and then said, "Any other problems?"

He took a moment to slide a plate toward her, then rounded the island. Her pragmatic approach to his story caused the tension that had built in his muscles to dissipate with each step. For perhaps the first time, the story seemed to belong to the past, and could be discussed with a certain amount of detachment.

"A broken arm," he replied to her question, as he sat on the stool next to hers and reached for the fried rice. "And they discovered I had nonstructural scoliosis."

Following his lead, she started piling food onto her plate. "Cause?"

"Inflammation. It was successfully treated."

For a while they concentrated on eating, but Cort could almost hear the wheels turning in her head. Liz Prudhomme wasn't the type to let a conversation like this just drop. Not if she was really interested.

So it wasn't a surprise when she finally asked, "Were you adopted?"

"Nope." That also didn't sting so much anymore, although when he'd been a teenager it had. "I ended up aging out of the foster-care system."

She nodded. "Nowadays there would be all kinds of posts on social media, people lining up to adopt you. Back then, not so much." The glance she sent him had warmth rushing down his spine, although he didn't know why. "You made it through the system, though, and all the way to success. That takes guts and determination."

He couldn't hold her gaze, pleasure at her praise making him turn away. Looking down at his plate and wrestling with a particularly slippery tangle of noodles was a welcome distraction. Getting them into his mouth and chewing also put off the need to reply until the unexpected rush of emotion subsided. "I had help."

"Really?" When he looked at her out of the corner of his eye, Liz was no longer watching him but helping herself to more food. "That's unusual in the foster-care system, or so I've heard."

"Yes, well, some of my foster families were good people." Not all, but he didn't want to go there. "But it was a couple of teachers who really got me on the right track at the right time." When she made an interested sound in the back of her throat, he continued. "I had a football coach who kept at me until I joined the school's officer trainer program, and a science teacher who saw something in me I didn't see in myself. She suggested I consider medicine." Even now, the memory made him laugh. "Imagine a scruffy, angry teenager in dirty, too-small clothes being told he should aspire to be a doctor. I told her she was nuts, but she persisted and the two things, the training program and her insistence, came together in the end."

When he least expected it, she sent him another of those clear-eyed looks. "Somewhere along the line your own determination had to come into play. No matter what anyone else says to a person, if they're not committed to a goal they won't make it." She mimed doffing a hat. "Kudos to you."

What could he say to that? Desperation had been his initial driver, but he doubted she'd understand the life he'd lived, so he just sketched her a bow and saw her lips quirk with her version of a smile.

"The army played a huge role too."

"You sound almost nostalgic about the service. Why'd you leave?"

Memories, like noxious smoke, suddenly filled his head, and had to be forced away. Keeping his gaze on his plate, he said, "It was time." Knowing how abrupt it sounded, he forced a smile and asked, "What about you? How did you end up in medicine?"

She shrugged, pushing away her plate, but there was an infinitesimal tightening of the skin around her mouth before she replied, "I knew from when I was a child what I wanted to do."

"And no one was talking you out of it, huh?"

He said it as a joke, but the way she nodded told him there was a lot more to the story. "Hell, no." When she met his gaze, her eyes were gleaming with the laughter she hardly ever allowed to escape. "Many tried, none succeeded."

Desire stabbed through him, shocking in its swiftness and intensity. It was the twinkle in her eyes, her candid acknowledgement of her strength of will, and, he admitted to himself, the easy way she'd heard and taken in his story. No drama, or false sympathy. It all just made him want her with the same ferocity he'd felt when knowing they only had a few minutes to be together in the hospital. And now remembering they had all night heightened his arousal. His need.

It must have shown on his face, because her eyes got slumberous, her lips softened, and a hint of color touched her cheeks and the tips of her ears. It made him want to tease her, much as he had the night they'd spent together in Mexico. That night had seemed to stretch to infinity, redolent with soft gasps and hot kisses, the intimate stroke of hands and lips across skin, the rise of unstoppable passion.

Getting up, he held out his hand to her.

"Come, let's go sit on the couch, maybe watch a movie."

Those eloquent eyebrows twitched, and her eyelids drooped farther. "Sure," she said, and took his hand with no hint of hesitation.

His heart leapt at that calm acceptance.

Tugging her to her feet, he let go of her hand to unbutton her sweater. "Make sure you watch the movie carefully, no matter what happens," he said. "There will be a test later."

"Ha-ha-ha," was her reply, but there was a breathy quality to her voice that told him she knew exactly what kind of distraction he planned. "And what kind of reward will I get if I get all the answers right?"

Leaning in close as he slid the sweater off her body, he whispered into her ear, and got his own reward when a pleasure-drenched little sound broke from her throat.

"I'll pay really close attention." It was an amusement-laden croak. "I want my prize."

"Good." He started on the button of her jeans, excitement firing across his flesh as he anticipated making her climax over and over again. "I want you to have it."

Want you to have it all.

CHAPTER NINE

SHE WANTED TO STAY.

Liz lay still beside Cort, trying to convince herself to get up and go home.

Staying the night had never been part of the deal.

It smacked of that *more* she'd promised herself to avoid at all costs.

Yet his bed was comfortable and, so far, there was no snoring to disturb the quiet of his apartment. Coming from outside, the hum of traffic, muted by gently falling snow, was also having a soporific effect.

She forced her eyes open to stare at the window, which was covered by light sheers, while she catalogued the pleasant aches caused by Cort's incredible lovemaking.

Sex. It was wonderful, but just sex.

A shiver crept up her arms, making her nipples bead. Whatever she called it, it was fantastic. Something about looking into those eyes, dark with passion, intent on her, elevated the experience from purely physical to something she didn't want to think about, much less name. Just the thought of it brought a sheen of anxious sweat to her forehead.

So, instead, she thought about what he'd told her about his beginnings, and how he'd ended up a surgeon. Knowing where he'd come from to become the man he was filled her with admiration. And that didn't even include whatever it was that had caused him to leave the service. There was a story there, one he'd shied away from telling, which probably meant it was really bad.

She doubted she would have survived, much less thrived the way he had.

The man in question rolled over onto his side to face her. Immediately her body quickened, tingles racing through her belly to settle between her thighs.

He made her so greedy.

So when he reached for her, pulled her close, she didn't resist, even though her head was telling her to. And when he kissed her, his hand slicking across her skin again to find a spot she hadn't even known was an erogenous zone until he'd shown her it was, she melted, gave in once more.

Later, floating down from the high he'd taken her on, she again thought about leaving, convinced herself she'd do it in a couple of minutes.

"There's something I have to say."

Liz braced herself, ready to get up and go if he made some fatuous comment about the sex, or spouted some romantic nonsense. So she made her tone cool as she asked, "What?"

"I'm starving."

That was so unexpected it startled a chuckle from her throat before she could stop it. Then her stomach rumbled, as though in agreement, and he laughed too.

Liz replied, "I guess I am too. What do you feel like having?"

She was thinking about the leftover Chinese in the kitchen, but Cort had other ideas.

"Arepas," he said promptly, following it with a little hum, as though already tasting them. "I haven't had a really good pulled pork *arepa* sandwich since I got here."

Now, that was something she could help with. Her love of food was well known among her intimates, and one of her favorites was Hispanic food in all its various incarnations.

"Colombian or Venezuelan?" Already she was running through a list of her favorite spots, trying to figure out which was closest.

"Mmm, Colombian for preference, although both are delicious."

Liz bounced out of bed to start looking for her scattered clothes. "Great, because there's a place about ten blocks from here that sells the most amazing Colombian food you've ever tasted outside Bogotá."

"Isn't it kind of late?"

Liz glanced at her watch, and then gave him a wrinkled brow look. He was still lying in bed, his arms crossed behind his head, as relaxed as anything.

And so delicious her insides melted a little.

Having that broad chest on display in front of her almost made her give up her planned excursion and hop back into bed, but once set on a course it usually took a stick of dynamite to divert her.

Hands planted on her hips, she asked, "Are you kidding? This is New York City. Whatever you want to eat, whenever you want to eat it, you can find a place, and I know most of them. You coming with me or what?"

"All right, all right. Don't get bent out of shape," he grumbled, as he swung his legs out of bed, making her mouth water.

And not for the promised food.

He strolled over to his chest of drawers, looking back at her over his shoulder. "I was enjoying the sight of you running around looking for your clothes."

"Ha-ha," she replied, heading for the bathroom and not mentioning how much she had enjoyed the view of him emerging from under the covers like some mythic god rising from the sea.

The night was cold. The earlier fluffy snow had morphed into small, stinging bits of ice, and Liz and Cort spent much of the journey to the restaurant talking about the never-ending winter and wondering if spring would ever arrive. They agreed the flu outbreak seemed to have slowed, but if the weather continued to be cold, it could pick up again.

The small restaurant, La Tortuga Roja, was down a short alley off a main road, and not visible from the sidewalk. While the outside seemed grubby, the inside was clean and simply decorated, and it was full.

Cort looked around with obvious surprise.

"I guess I wasn't the only person craving *arepas*," he remarked.

"Apparently not," she replied, leading the way to the only available booth.

After the waitress had brought menus and taken their drink orders, Cort asked, "How do you know about this place?"

"I like food." There was the familiar nagging shame she'd been fighting her entire life, but she just lifted her chin and continued, "I always try to find the best restaurants I can for the different types of food I like, usually by asking someone who comes from the country or region where it's native."

"That makes sense." He was looking at the menu, a little line between his brows. "I love food too, although I'll be the first to tell you I can be picky."

"I'd have thought the army would have cured you of that."

He glanced up, a smile lighting his face. "Not even the foster-care system cured me of being picky."

He spoke so easily about what had to have been a difficult and perhaps frightening childhood. That, along with the knowledge their relationship had a predetermined shelf life, caused Liz to open up in a way she normally wouldn't.

"I had a love-hate relationship with food when I was young, now it's just a love affair."

Cort's gaze sharpened. "Love-hate? As in an eating disorder?"

It felt good to talk about it. She never did, but he somehow made it easy to reply. "Looking back on it now, as a medical practitioner, I don't think I was there yet. I was, however, doing unhealthy things, trying to achieve unrealistic goals and make other people happy."

Her mother had never overtly said anything, but there had been others not so kind. *Are you sure you want another piece? Oh, you've put on so much weight.* She'd compared her chunky, preteen self to the girls in her class and to her waif-thin mother, and had felt inadequate.

"How old were you?"

Liz closed her menu, having decided what she wanted to eat. "It was between the ages of about ten and fourteen. I take after my father's side of the family, who are all big, raw-boned people.

My mother, on the other hand, had a tiny Japanese grandmother, and the rest of her family isn't much bigger. I know she must still look at me and wonder how she produced such a huge human."

She could say it with amusement now, but when she'd been the fat kid at school, taunted by the other girls, picked on by the boys, it had been anything but funny. Not even the knowledge that she was smart and capable and had wanted to be a doctor had made her not long to fit in. Or taken away the need to see admiration in her mother's eyes. Just being a straight A student hadn't seemed enough.

"What changed?"

"Now, that's a story in itself."

Just then the waitress brought their drinks and, since they'd both decided what they wanted, took their orders. As soon as she walked away, Cort said, "So, what happened?"

Liz let a little smile pull at her lips. His enthusiastic interest was pretty cute.

"My mother started talking about my debutante ball."

His brow wrinkled slightly. "Not sure I know what that is."

"Lucky you. It's just a big formal dance where very rich people put their daughters on parade. At least, that's how I see it. My mom, however, was far more excited. She didn't know what was happening to me in school, how the same girls I was going to have to go to the ball with despised me, and I despised them. Just the thought of having to wear a ballgown made me want to break out in hives."

Cort's eyebrows lifted. "Come on, it couldn't have been that bad."

"At the time it felt like they were opening the gates of hell and telling me to step in. Truthfully, I was so scared of having everyone compare me to the other girls, seeing how much bigger I was than them, how different I looked."

Or being compared to her mother, who'd won beauty contests and been voted "Most Popular" in school. By every measure, except scholastically, Liz had seen herself as a failure.

"Now I realize I was frightened, but back then I convinced myself I was taking a stand for feminism and equality. I told my parents I didn't want to go to a ball, I wanted to be a doctor, and doctors didn't need to be debs."

Cort was actually leaning forward, his elbows

on the table, his intent gaze fixed on her face. "How did that go down?"

She chuckled. "Like a lead balloon. They tried to reason with me, but I was terrified and determined and wouldn't give in. The one good thing to come out of it was that they sent me to boarding school in England the next school year."

"Why'd they do that?" Cort sounded both perplexed and a little angry. "What did they hope to achieve?"

"Not sure. I never asked, but being there, meeting new people just as I started to grow into my body, made all the difference in my confidence. For the first time in my life I knew no one was comparing me to my mother, or expecting me to be anyone other than I was. The friends I made then are still my best ones, because they accepted me exactly as I was."

Of course, her transformation hadn't happened overnight, and it had taken Andrew to completely cure her of the urge to try to change to please others. He'd reiterated all the bad things she'd felt her parents thought about her, and she'd realized that if she didn't accept herself the way she was, she'd never be happy in her skin.

A shadow crossed Cort's face, the corners of

his mouth dipping down for an instant, before he said, "Yeah, having friends is important, especially at that age."

Another story she itched to hear, yet something in his eyes made her hesitate to ask. Instead, as the waitress approached with a groaning tray, she said, "Oh, good, here comes our food."

And thereafter the conversation turned to other, less personal things, while her curiosity simmered in the back of her mind. Cort Smith was turning out to be far more interesting than she could ever have imagined, even outside the bedroom.

Cort had a hard time believing he was sitting across from a totally relaxed Liz Prudhomme at ten o'clock on a Friday night, eating an *arepa* stuffed with *lechona*. As he took a bite of his sandwich, the delicious pork filling practically melting in his mouth, he watched Liz help herself to a sampling of the various dishes on the table— *arroz con coco*, *carne asado* and *tostones*, as well as *arepas* to go with it all.

He contemplated what she'd revealed about her childhood, having a difficult time picturing her as an outcast in any setting. Now, as an adult, her confidence seemed unassailable but clearly it hadn't always been that way.

Knowing she came from a wealthy family, if he'd thought about her childhood at all he'd have guessed she'd always been surrounded by admiring friends who'd wanted to be just like her. Probably a letter athlete and class president as well, like the star of a teen movie of the week.

Just went to show you really couldn't judge what a person's life had been just from outward appearances.

Hearing that little bit of personal information made him hungry for more. From the moment they'd met in Mexico, Liz had proven herself adept at getting him to talk about his life without revealing much about hers. Despite how easily she was divulging information now, he figured he'd have to be careful not to have her clam up on him again. He knew, without a doubt, she wouldn't hesitate to cut him off at the knees if she thought he was overstepping his bounds.

Swallowing the bite he'd been chewing on, he said, "If this food is any indication of your standards, you're going to have to give me a list of places to eat at."

"It's really good, isn't it?" She pointed to the beef. "Have some."

Snagging a piece, as directed, he asked, "So, have you lived in New York all your life?"

The look she gave him was one of amusement. "Do I sound like a New Yorker? No, I'm from the San Francisco Bay area. That's where my parents still live."

"How come you didn't go back there after your residency?" If he had a family, real roots in a community, that would probably be what he'd do.

Liz shrugged one shoulder, and for a moment he thought she wasn't going to answer, then she replied, "It's complicated."

She took another bite of food and chewed, leaving him to wonder if that was all the answer he was going to get. After she swallowed, then took a sip of her iced tea, she said, "Truthfully, I spent a lot more happy times here in New York than I did back home. Those two aunts I was named for asked for me to come to spend part of summer with them when I got into my teens, and my parents insisted I go. At first, it felt like another punishment, but those two old ladies were amazing and I looked forward to those weeks every year. I fell in love with New York and now there's nowhere I'd rather be."

He wanted to dig deeper, feeling there was more to it than just that, but before he could formulate his next question, she continued.

"What do you think of New York? What have you seen and done since you got here?"

Deflected again, and yet he couldn't really blame her. Theirs wasn't the type of relationship that inspired confidences. They weren't looking to get to know each other too deeply, just enjoy the attraction.

"I like it, so far. Took some time to get used to the pace of the city, and the noise, but I'm enjoying exploring. Did some touristy things, like the Empire State Building, and Liberty and Ellis Island, but besides that I've just been nosing around a bit."

"If you're only going to be in New York for a fairly short time, you need to cram as much in as possible." She raised one eyebrow. "What are you into, besides martial arts and traveling?"

Her question made him have to think. For the last five years he'd been struggling to get back into civilian life without his best friend to do things with. It suddenly struck him how much he'd deferred to Mimi's wants when it had come to what they'd done together.

"I like live music, but not at big venues. I used to play a lot of pool, and miss it. Just checking out different neighborhoods, seeing how other people live and have fun, that's how I usually try to get to know a city."

With her wealthy background that probably sounded boring and pedestrian to Liz, but he wasn't going to present himself as anything other than what he was. He was a simple man, with pretty simple tastes and interests. Racking his brain, he continued with his list of things he liked to do.

"Usually when I travel I go to natural history museums, and rent a motorbike to look at the countryside. I'm looking forward to exploring outside the city on my bike when the weather gets nice."

It was as though a curtain came down, and the relaxed, almost smiling Liz disappeared in an instant. She looked down and pushed her plate aside.

"Well, you won't lack for things to do and see here. If you need any suggestions, let me know."

As was often the case, he was left wondering

what had cause her abrupt change of mood. Was it because she'd suddenly realized just how incredibly boring he was?

When she glanced at her watch, he knew the evening, which he'd been enjoying so much, was coming to an end. He didn't want it to. Instead, he wanted to ask her to come back home with him, spend the night. Seeing her so laid back and obviously enjoying her food had made him hungry for her again. Just one look at her closed-off expression and veiled eyes told him it would be useless to ask.

But there was one thing he had to say before they parted ways. Catching the waitress's eye, he motioned for the bill, then said to Liz, "I definitely want suggestions, so make me a list of must-sees. Better yet, show me around yourself. You love the city, so I have no doubt you know all the best places, and the best times to go to them."

That earned him one of her sharp, solemn glances.

"I'll think about it," she said, turning to pull her coat off the back of the chair.

And he was smart enough to leave it at that.

CHAPTER TEN

LIZ LEFT CORT standing on the sidewalk outside the restaurant and jumped into a cab to head home. All the fun and enjoyment she'd felt in his company had drained away at the mention of the motorcycle, and she had to wonder why her taste in men was so predictable. The more time she spent with Cort, the more he reminded her of Andrew, as if one man hooked on adventure and the need for speed wasn't enough.

At least they didn't look alike, at all. Andrew had been blond and sleek, with a swimmer's physique, while Cort was more the epitome of tall, dark and handsome. A solid man, built for holding a woman in such a way that she felt safe. Protected.

Not that she needed protection. She was more than capable of protecting herself, thank you very much! Yet when Cort held her the very center of her feminine core was touched, and she felt beautiful.

But the mention of the motorbike had made her blood run cold.

When she'd first started going out with Andrew, she had ridden on the back of his bike all the time. Although he'd had a car, it had been his favorite way of getting around and Liz, not having had much experience with motorcycles, hadn't minded until after the late fall night when they'd crashed. Luckily for her all she'd sustained had been some painful road rash and a slight concussion. Andrew had broken his arm. Had it been her with the broken ulna and radius, she'd have had to miss a key part of her practical anatomy course, and that had been a nonstarter for her.

"Come on, Liz," Andrew had wheedled. "It's like riding a horse. You have to get right back on. It'll be fine. The odds of having another accident are astronomical."

Much as she'd wanted to demand he show her those statistics, she hadn't bothered. It wouldn't have changed her mind. The thought of how close she'd come to losing a year of schooling had been like a shock of cold water to her system, not to mention how close they'd come to real disaster.

Andrew had slowed considerably just prior to going around the corner and having the back tire slide out from under them. Usually he'd ridden like a madman, going at phenomenal speeds. If he'd been running true to form, she had no doubt they'd both be dead.

It had been the end of her riding pillion on his bike.

And perhaps the beginning of the end of their relationship.

Sometimes she tried to tell herself that she'd just matured faster than he had, but she knew in her heart it wasn't true. Andrew probably wouldn't have changed and, while perhaps it made her a hypocrite to be mad at him for wanting her to change, she'd hoped *he* would. She'd had her life mapped out, at least roughly, and she'd longed for his approval of her plans. Instead, he'd wanted her to put her dream of being a doctor on hold, had treated it as though it hadn't been important.

"You can always go back to it," he'd said, as he'd laid maps of Europe, already marked with routes he planned to take, out on her kitchen table. "We're young, and this is the time to travel and see the world, not when we're too old to enjoy it."

She'd been tempted. Oh, yes, she had. When faced with the choice of losing him or going with him, she'd hesitated. Each had tried to convince the other their way was the best, Andrew arguing for her to take a year or two off, Liz arguing for him to wait until she was through with her studies.

Eventually it hadn't mattered. While she'd been looking into what it would mean to put her school career on hiatus, Andrew had decided he didn't want her to go.

"We've had some good times, Liz, but you're not spontaneous enough for me. Sometimes I wonder if you really have feelings for me at all because, if you do, you don't show it. I think it will be better if I make the trip on my own."

It hadn't been fair, at all, what he'd been saying. She'd tried to be more like him, dropping everything to go out even when she'd known she shouldn't, staying out later than she should, even occasionally missing a class because Andrew had wanted to ride down to the sea or go to a concert. The difference was she'd wanted to succeed and had known she couldn't do well if she constantly did those things. So sometimes she'd tell him no, and it had never gone over well, but she'd stuck to her guns. Just as she had with not riding the motorcycle anymore.

Better to be useful than decorative.

Don't allow your father, or any man, to dictate to you.

Leaning her head back in the taxi, Liz brooded on those words. She still believed in what Nanny Hardy and her great-aunts had said, and honestly felt if it hadn't been for their wise words, she'd have thrown it all over for Andrew.

And probably would have died with him during an early snowfall in Germany, when he'd destroyed his bike on a lonely road, too far away for help to get to him in time.

Her love for Andrew had made her so weak, it was frightening. The irony that his change of heart had been the only thing that had stopped her from throwing everything away she'd fought for hadn't been lost on her, but hadn't made it hurt any less.

For a moment, before she got herself under control, her eyes stung with the tears she'd steadfastly refused to allow to fall for all these years.

Stupid for it all to be coming back to the surface after all this time, interfering with what should be a good time with a man she already knew was transient in her life, and therefore safe. Better to put it out of her mind, once and for all, and just enjoy the amazing sex and Cort's company, which was surprisingly easy, and casual enough to not make her want to run.

He wanted to see New York, and had been right when he'd said she could show it to him in a way most other people couldn't.

She could see no harm in that and, if she was being scrupulously honest with herself, she wanted to enjoy him for as long as he stuck around, especially now she was pretty sure he wouldn't make something out of it that wasn't there.

Pulling out her tablet, she started typing in a list of places she'd take him, and things he should do, at least once, while he was there.

It should be fun.

Right?

Standing outside the Colombian restaurant and watching Liz's taxi drive away, Cort was sure it was the last time they would go anywhere together. Her change of attitude after asking him what he liked made him sure he wasn't interesting enough for her, and not worth bothering about.

It turned out he was wrong.

She actually approached him the following day with a list of things to do, and a plan for how and when they'd do them.

Liz Prudhomme was nothing if not organized.

Well, except for her locker.

Looking down at her tablet, where he could see an extensive list, she said, "There are some things we'll leave for when the weather gets better, like the New York Botanical Garden, Coney Island and Governors Island, but there are so many other things to do, you won't be bored."

And now, as they walked along a sidewalk in the East Village, he had to admit she was right. He'd been anything but bored. They'd become workout buddies when he'd complained about the gym near his house not being open twenty-four hours a day, and she kept him on his toes when they went at the same time. She'd taken him through the Arms and Armor Department at the Metropolitan Museum, to a play Off-Off-Broadway and a musical on Broadway. In between there had been a variety of food, a martial arts tournament, and a number of nights at clubs listening to blues, country, and indie performers.

The breadth of Liz's interests and knowledge was amazing.

Cort looked back at the venue they'd just left, where people still trickled out into the night.

"What did you say that was we just watched again?"

"A poetry slam," she replied, giving him an amused glance. "I'm guessing it's your first?"

That made him chuckle. She knew it was, if only from the way he'd sat there with his mouth hanging open. It had been one of the most wonderful things he'd seen.

"Some of those poets were like listening to the blues being spoken, rather than sung."

She stopped in the middle of the sidewalk and stared at him in such a strange way he felt self-conscious.

"I guess that didn't make any sense," he said quickly, but she interrupted him with an uplifted hand.

"On the contrary, that's the best description I've heard in a long time. I'd never have guessed you had the soul of an aesthete."

The back of his neck got warm, although he

wasn't sure whether it was with embarrassment or pleasure. All he knew was that he had to laugh it off somehow.

"Ah, so you thought I was just a Philistine, huh?"

The corners of her lips twitched, her mouth softening into her version of a smile. When she started walking again, he fell into step beside her once more. "Actually, the Philistines were highly cultured. It's one of those pieces of misinformation that gets passed down because the victors always get to write the history."

They walked for a while more, discussing the poetry slam and their favorite performers, until they came to a well-lit pool hall. Cort turned to her, raising his eyebrows.

"Pool?"

She shrugged. "You said you liked to play, so I figured you could teach me. Neither of us work early tomorrow, so we can stay out a little longer."

"Sure," he said, surprised she'd even remembered he'd said it.

For a Wednesday night there were quite a few people in the club, which also had an arcade and dartboards.

"Now, if you want to give me a fighting chance of winning, we could play darts," Liz said.

"Next time," Cort said, pulling out money to feed into the pool table. "It feels good to find something you're not an expert at."

Liz snorted, watching as he racked up the balls. When he was finished and selected a couple of cues, he started his instructions, telling her the basics and then showing her the break. A solid ball went into a pocket, and he stopped to explain that, since he'd sunk that one, it was up to him to sink all the other solids, before sinking the eight ball.

"So when do I play?"

"If I miss a shot, you're up."

She sighed, as though they'd been there for an hour rather than ten minutes. Realizing she was getting bored, he intentionally missed the next shot.

"Your turn," he said. "You need to sink the striped balls."

Liz gave the table a skeptical glance. "In any particular order?"

"Nope," he replied.

"Okay," she said. "This'll be a short turn, so get ready to play again."

She awkwardly tried to set up for a shot, holding the cue short and too far away from her body.

"Hang on," he said. "Will you let me help you?"

"I suppose," she huffed.

Chuckling at how much she obviously despised being at a disadvantage, he moved to stand behind her, putting his hand between her shoulder blades and gently pushing her lower.

"Bend over further."

"As the bishop said to the actress," she muttered.

"What?"

"Never mind. I'll explain later."

She always came out with little sayings he'd never heard before, mostly, he figured, because of the difference in their experiences and upbringings. He didn't mind, though, since she was broadening his horizons and giving him a whole new way of looking at things.

Instead of asking anything more, he leaned over, snuggling up to her bottom. It took all his concentration to help her position her arms, since being that close to her was so arousing.

His fascination with and attraction to her certainly hadn't waned. If anything, getting to know her better had made their continued intimate relationship even hotter, wilder.

And when she wiggled a little, shifting position, he almost groaned aloud.

Ignoring the erection pushing at the front of his jeans, he said, "Okay, aim for that red-striped ball there. Try to hit it a little to the left of center, so it goes into the side pocket."

"Easy for you to say."

He backed away, watching as she made a couple of practice feints. At least the hand she had on the felt looked to be in a good position. Most new players had a hard time with that...

Crack.

"All right! You sank it. See, that wasn't so hard, was it?"

The look she gave him made him smile, a smile that slowly faded to be replaced with a wide-eyed stare as she ran the table.

"Why you little..."

She shrugged, her eyes twinkling, a grin stretching her luscious lips.

"I'm sorry, I couldn't resist. My brother taught me to play years ago, and then wouldn't play with me anymore because I kept beating him."

Cort burst out laughing, going over to put some

more money in the table so they could play another game, trying to ignore how fast his heart was beating at the sight of her smile.

"Well, let's see how you do this time around."

He was actually still laughing when they left the pool hall an hour and a half later. He'd won two games, she'd won three, and they'd trash-talked each other the entire time. Even Liz had laughed out loud a couple of times.

Outside, the early-spring air was cool, but the sky was clear, an almost full moon hanging like a milky lamp above their heads. Cort had been around her long enough to know Liz didn't go for public displays of affection, didn't even like holding hands, and it didn't bother him. Not when he woke up every morning when she'd slept over at his place to find her draped over him, providing more coverage than his comforter.

But sometimes he needed her to know what she did to him, whether they were out in public or not.

As they came abreast of a closed shop, he swept her into a hug, and backed her into the darkness afforded by the recessed doorway. Her only reaction was a little gasp, and then he felt her melt against him.

"You make me crazy," he whispered into her ear, and was rewarded by her shiver. "I want you, right now."

She pressed against him, swiveled her hips in the way she knew made him go nuts. The attraction between them was always simmering just below the surface, waiting to explode into passion at a look, a touch, a whisper.

"I'll call for a taxi," she said, but neither of them made a move to disengage.

"In a minute," he said, looking over his shoulder at the almost deserted street. "I just want to…"

And he kissed her until she was making little noises in the back of her throat, and until he knew if they didn't get out of there soon, they might be arrested for indecent exposure.

"Are there any hotels nearby?" He growled it against her neck, pinched her nipple in the way she loved, rocking his leg up into the junction of her thighs.

Liz gasped, shuddered, and said, "A decent one, about two blocks west."

Forcing himself to let her go, he backed out of the doorway, the ache in his groin excruciating. Every time they were together was like the first time for him. Liz could turn him on by simply being.

"That'll work," he said, taking a deep breath. "Race you."

CHAPTER ELEVEN

Mᴀʏ ʜᴀᴅ ғɪɴᴀʟʟʏ brought the full promise of spring, with balmy weather and, most of the time, not enough rain to make it difficult to enjoy. Today, though, wasn't one of those days, as a front moved through the northeast, bringing thunderstorms and the occasional bout of hail.

The hospital renovations were getting closer to completion, and they were on no-intake for emergency and surgical patients as the technicians were moving equipment into the newly arranged departments. Without the usual flood of patients, staff and visitors, those floors of the hospital had a ghost-town feel to them. Even Radiology was on a skeleton crew, with only one room open for use.

Liz was bored, taking the quiet time between non-emergency patients to catch up on paperwork and do some research she'd been putting off. She felt a little guilty at her secret glee when a young baseball player, whose attempt to slide into third had ended with a broken collarbone, came in for treatment. It really was a slow day when applying a figure eight bandage was as exciting as it got.

On her way back to the nurses' station, she saw Cort turn a corner ahead of her and come her way. Despite seeing him almost every day, her heart still did that little leap whenever he came into view, and the sight of his smiling face lifted her mood, no matter how testy she was feeling.

It really was a good thing he wouldn't be sticking around for too long. Already she'd been forced to acknowledge how easy it had been to get used to, and enjoy, his company.

Thank goodness there was no chance of falling for him.

She was smarter and stronger than that.

He paused next to her and casually asked, "Gym later?"

She was working early the next morning, so they didn't have anything else planned. She replied, "I was hoping it would be nice today so we could go for a run in Central Park, but the gym will have to do."

Cort stepped aside as a technician came by, wheeling an EKG monitor in front of him, the bulky machine taking up most of the hallway. The movement brought Cort closer to Liz, and her body reacted to the proximity, the now familiar sensation of arousal making her tingle, on the verge of shivering.

"Sounds good," he said. "I'm here for another hour and, for a change, there shouldn't be anything stopping me from leaving on time. So, say, six?"

For once they were actually on the same schedule, so it worked. "See you outside at six."

"Great." Cort gave her one of his knee-weakening grins, before heading off toward the elevators, leaving her standing there staring at his broad back as he walked away.

Tearing her gaze away from him, she looked blankly down at the clipboard in her hand, realizing that for the last couple of months they'd been more together than apart.

Yes, it really was a great thing that he was planning to move on in a few months. He would be so easy to get attached to.

Sometimes she thought, to be on the safe side, she should call a halt to whatever it was they had going on between them, yet just the thought of putting a stop to it made a sour spot grow in her stomach. Cort was easy to be around; fun to be with. Plus, he made her toes curl and her eyes cross in bed. She should just keep on enjoying it for as long as she could. On top of everything else, he still treated her as though she was a friend, never pushing for more or complaining if she turned down the opportunity for them to do something together. Giving her the space she needed to live her life.

It might sometimes feel like it was slipping out of control, but it was also perfect. Why mess with that?

Stuffing the clipboard under her arm, she rubbed her suddenly damp palms down the legs of her scrubs.

Yet she felt so conflicted. Wouldn't it be better to end the friendship now, rather than wait for the inevitable messy break-up to happen?

"Dr. Prudhomme?"

Startled out of her reverie, Liz pushed all the muddled, confusing thoughts from her mind. She'd think about Cort Smith, and how much space he was taking up in her head and life, later.

"Yes?" The intake nurse was holding the phone to her chest and looked frazzled, which was surprising on such a quiet day. "What is it?"

"I have a call from an ambulance a block away from here. They're taking a vehicle accident victim, male, twenty-five, with suspected brain injury, chest and abdominal trauma to Roosevelt, but there's been a water main break and they're stuck. The patient's crashing."

It couldn't happen at a worse time, with the hospital in such disarray, but Liz didn't hesitate.

"Tell them to bring him here, and get me a trauma team, stat."

"But, Doctor, I was told—"

"I don't care what you were told." Her veins were like ice now, her focus solely on saving the patient. "Tell them I'm waiting for them in the bay, and page the trauma team. Then get a medivac helicopter dispatched. As soon as we stabilize him, we're going to have to fly him to Roosevelt." She was already moving, heading to the entrance, the nurse's raised voice just a buzz of background noise.

There was one emergency room kept undisturbed for walk-ins and, although they'd all been told in no uncertain terms they weren't to take any trauma patients, Liz didn't care. They were the only chance the young man had to survive, and she'd do everything she could to save him.

Yet her stress levels went through the roof. This wasn't business as usual, not by a long shot, and she was aware of the risk she was taking with the patient's life.

Perhaps with her career at the hospital she truly loved.

She was shouting orders as she ran, and grabbed a surgical gown from a handy stack. Cold sweat beaded her skin under her scrubs, and she barely noticed the driving drizzle that hit her face when she crashed through the bay doors. A nurse came up behind her, reached out to tie the gown in place as Liz dragged on a pair of gloves.

Everything became a nightmarish blur as the ambulance seemed to take forever to enter the bay. They all rushed forward, Liz leading the charge, to open the doors to get at the patient. The gurney's wheels dropped to the ground with a clang, the sound reverberating in her chest, as she got her first look at the young man lying there, so perilously still.

Her gut clenched and for a sickening instant the edges of her vision grew dark.

Wheat-blond hair, a little too long, matted with blood. A hawkish nose prominent in the narrow, too-pale face. The motorcycle leathers, black with splashes of decorative blue.

Andrew.

Then reality returned, although her stomach continued to churn.

It wasn't Andrew, who, had he lived, would be in his midthirties now. It was just a young, desperately hurt young man who happened to look remarkably, almost horrifyingly, like him.

Even so, it took everything she had to gather her control, to take firm hold of her senses and the gurney as they ran back into the hospital, the paramedic in charge spewing information she somehow heard and absorbed over the clamor of her heartbeat. OS rate, BP, the horrifying list of known injuries, which made a hole of despair open in her stomach. Even if they had been functioning at full capacity, just from the severity of his wounds his chances of survival were slim.

Into the emergency room, Liz giving the count to hoist him onto the stretcher, beginning her examination even as the nurses were cutting his blood-soaked motorcycle leathers away, inserting the IVs and then administering Ringer's at her command.

Steady. Steady. Focus.

Put everything else aside and focus.

But even as she admonished herself, her gaze went back to the young man's face, and her heart contracted with pain.

"Should we remove the neck brace, Doctor?"

"No," Liz replied, swallowing against the sick taste rising at the back of her throat, doing everything she could to sound normal. "He's going to be flown to Roosevelt. Keep it on."

It made completing her examination more difficult, but taking it off and putting it back on would only increase the risk of exacerbating any potential neck injury.

His breathing was ragged, shallow, his oxygen saturation so low it was at near critical levels.

"I'm going to intubate."

She stuck out her hand and closed her fingers around the laryngoscope when the nurse slapped it into her palm. Moving to the head of the stretcher, she tilted his head back. When she opened his mouth and inserted the laryngoscope, her heart sank even further. Bloody mucus obscured her view.

"Suction."

How calm her voice sounded, in contrast to the

desperate chant in her head. *Hang on. Hang on. Hang on. We can save you if you just hang on.*

There. Now she could see a clear path down the trachea. "Eight-point-five millimeter," she said, sticking out her hand for the endotracheal tube. The brief spurt of relief she felt when the patient was properly intubated and she resumed her examination didn't last long.

Depressed skull fracture. Pupils responsive but sluggish. Broken ribs and suspected sternal fracture. Muffled heart sounds. Bruising forming on his abdomen. Severely broken femur.

And that was just for a start. Just what she could see in this first examination.

"Blood pressure dropping, Doctor. Eighty over sixty."

"I suspect cardiac tamponade. Portable ultrasound."

She'd been distantly aware of Dr. Yuen, who'd come in and had been doing his own examination of the patient, but she'd been too focused on her own to even look up. Now, hearing his words, she moved to the left side of the exam table in order to see the ultrasound screen. The surgeon squirted gel on the patient's chest, then started running the wand over the area. Liz watched, seeing the heart beating frantically, trying to keep working although surrounded by blood.

"Pericardiocentesis kit."

Liz gave the order, but Dr. Yuen said, "I've got it, Dr. Prudhomme."

"Yes, Dr. Yuen." But she stayed in place, ready to assist should he need it.

Another nurse came in, and said, "The 'copter should be here in ten minutes."

Dr. Yuen froze for a moment, his hands poised over the patient, whether from the nurse's words or from some reluctance to do the procedure, Liz didn't know.

"Dr. Yuen, either you insert that tube, stat, or I will."

The fierceness in her tone drew the younger man's gaze for an instant, his eyes wide behind the splatter mask, and then he turned back to the patient.

Cort stood against the wall, staying out of everyone's way, observing the team working to stabilize the young accident victim. There was really so little going on otherwise that when the call had come for a trauma team, he'd come down, even though he'd known Dr. Yuen would probably beat him to it.

Now tension tightened the back of his neck as he watched the young surgeon perform the pericardiocentesis.

There was something wrong with Liz, with her reactions, the way she was moving. He'd had ample experience of working with her, so it was easy to recognize the difference between her usual way of behaving and what he was seeing.

She looked pale to him, and her movements were choppy, although he could discern no lowering in the standard of care she was providing for the patient. But it was the way she was hovering over Dr. Yuen, almost crowding the young surgeon and snapping at him to do the procedure that was most surprising.

Then she turned to one of the nurses and said, "Make sure Roosevelt has a neurosurgeon on standby when the helicopter lands."

"I've got it under control, Dr. Prudhomme." Dr. Yuen's voice held a hint of steel. "Nurse Hayes, watch that line."

As the team worked in tandem to stabilize the young man, Cort kept his gaze on Liz, becoming more convinced there was something going on with her.

"Helicopter is here," someone called out.

Liz checked to make sure the endotracheal tube and IV lines were properly secured for transport while Dr. Yuen checked the pressure cuff surrounding the young man's leg.

With one more check of the young man's vitals, Yuen said, "He's as stable as he's going to get. Let's get him on the transport board."

The team checked and rechecked the lines and tubes, clearing any in jeopardy of being displaced by the move, and then, on Yuen's count of three, transferred the patient onto the board. Once he was strapped down, covered to keep him warm, and everything had been checked once more, they were moving, heading for the roof.

Cort hung back, but instead of following them to the nearest elevators, he ran to the bank on the other side of the ER. By the time he got to the roof observation area it was to see the patient being transferred over to the flight crew, Dr. Yuen going along to monitor the young man en route.

The rest of the trauma and ER team members

turned and came back inside, chatting amongst themselves, but Liz stood watching as the patient was loaded. And she still didn't move when the helicopter took off, the rotors kicking up a cloud of dust and swirling rain, or after the aircraft disappeared into the New York skyline.

There was a slump to her shoulders and her fingers were fisted so tightly that even from a distance Cort could see her knuckles were white.

She looked so defeated Cort's chest ached just looking at her. Knowing her, she probably wanted to be alone, but he couldn't just walk away and leave her without trying to find out what was going on.

Even if she rejected his interference, and him.

CHAPTER TWELVE

IT WASN'T UNTIL he got out to the helipad and next to her that he realized she was crying, tears streaming down her face, her body shaking with stifled sobs.

"Liz—"

"Go away, Cort."

She said it fiercely, but there was no mistaking the pain in her voice, the hitch between the words. Part of him wanted to honor her request, turn away from the hurt of being shut out that way, but somehow, now he was standing beside her, that wasn't an option.

"I can't. Not when you're like this. Talk to me, Liz. Let me help if I can."

He was confused, unsure of what was upsetting her so much. From what he'd seen, the young patient's prognosis was poor. There had been signs of abnormal posturing, which often indicated a less-than-happy outcome. Yet this was something all ER doctors and trauma surgeons faced. As much as they wanted to, they couldn't save everyone and Liz's reaction to this patient was more intense than any he'd seen her display before.

"I don't need help."

"Everyone needs help at one time or another, even if it's just a shoulder to lean on or an ear to listen."

Still she hesitated, taking deep breaths, obviously trying to stem her tears.

"Please, let me help in whatever way I can."

"There's nothing you can do," she finally said, swiping her sleeve across her face. "It's just ghosts."

"Ghosts? What kind of ghosts?"

She exhaled hard, through her mouth, and shook her head. "Once, a long time ago, I knew... someone. He died in a motorcycle accident in Germany. I've been thinking about him a lot recently, and when I saw that patient..."

"He reminded you of your friend."

Liz nodded; just a sharp dip of her chin. "He even looked like Andrew. It...threw me."

The knowledge came to him in a flash, made a sour taste tickle the back of his throat. "You loved him."

"Yes."

It was a stark admission, almost resentful, and Cort remembered her indictment of love, her definition of it as a terminal disease that weakened the brain. His stomach churned as he realized Liz was still in love with this man Andrew.

Yet he had to put his muddled feelings aside, concentrate on doing whatever he could to ease Liz's distress.

But what could he say? What could anyone say to alleviate her pain?

"I'm so sorry, Liz."

She bit her lower lip then let it go on a hard exhalation. And, as if the rush of air somehow released the words, said, "He always rode too fast, took too many chances. But it was a long time ago. I should be over it by now."

Now he finally understood why, during their time in the Colombian restaurant, she'd withdrawn when he'd mentioned his motorcycle. There was no doubt bikes and riding held nothing but bad memories for her. Time didn't heal all wounds, he knew that from hard experience, so he gently touched her shoulder, needing her to know she wasn't alone.

"It's not something you can get over, I guess. You just learn to live with it."

She turned to him so suddenly he wasn't expecting it, but when she gripped the front of his shirt with both hands and buried her face in his neck, he pulled her in tighter, embracing her.

Wanting to shelter her from the pain.

She was trembling, her agony a physical thing.

"We'd argued," she whispered, almost too low to hear. "He wanted to see the world. I wanted to finish med school. I was supposed to go with him, was on the verge of saying yes, but he decided he wanted to go alone. Didn't want me to go with him."

"Why?"

"He wanted to tour Europe on his bike, but we'd had an accident the year before, and I wouldn't ride with him anymore. We were so mean to each other, Cort, saying cruel things. Then he left. I was a little relieved because then I didn't have to put my studies on hold, but I always thought there would be time to make it up. There wasn't. That was the last time I saw him."

Cort was at a loss as to what to say. To him, it sounded as though her Andrew had been a selfish man who hadn't deserved Liz's love, but he certainly couldn't say that. He wasn't sure if he should push for more information either, afraid Liz would clam up on him, but he had to say *something*.

"Was he a doctor too?"

Liz sniffled, the sound heartbreaking Cort tightened his hold on her, pressed her close, wishing there was more he could do.

"Yes. He was a year ahead of me, but medicine wasn't a calling for him, more of an expectation, since his father was a doctor and hoped Andrew would take over his practice one day. Andrew was smart, but just scraped through. He wasn't dedicated, you know?"

No doubt that had been another bone of contention between them, Cort thought. Liz wasn't the kind to do anything half-heartedly. She would have been determined to be at the top of her class.

She sighed. "I know it's wrong to second-guess everything, but it's hard not to think about what might have been if the choices we'd made had been different."

That he could understand but, at the same time, she had to stop beating herself up over someone else's decisions.

"That's true, but if you'd gone with him, you might not have survived the accident either."

Just saying the words made his heart contract, filled the pit of his stomach with an icy ball.

"Or I might have convinced him not to be on the road when a snowstorm had been forecast. Or…"

"Or what?" he asked, hearing deepening pain in her tone. "Or what, Liz?"

"Or I might have been able to keep him alive until they got him to hospital."

There. Now he knew the crux of her agony. Recognized it far more clearly than she could ever imagine.

"Survivor's guilt, doctor edition," he said quietly. "I completely understand."

"Do you?" she asked, lifting her head to search his face.

"Oh, yes."

"Tell me."

He never spoke about Brody with anyone except with Jenna, and had never, ever mentioned his feelings of guilt to Brody's wife. But this was different. Liz needed to know she wasn't the only one who had those kinds of feelings.

"My best friend died almost six years ago from

a prescription drug overdose. He worked construction and I knew he'd hurt his back a couple years before, but it didn't even occur to me he might be hooked on painkillers. Despite the fact he'd hidden it even from his wife, I can't get over the guilt of thinking I should have known, should have been able to help him."

"Were you already back home then?"

"No, I was still posted overseas."

"So, if he didn't want anyone to know, why do you think you could have helped him?"

The pain around his heart intensified. He didn't want to talk about it anymore, but she'd opened up to him and deep down inside he wanted her to understand how hurtful it had been.

Still was.

"I learned early not to get attached to anyone, Liz. When you get passed from one foster home to another, you get a clear understanding of how impermanent everything in life really is. But Brody… Brody was different. We were fourteen when we met, and we were like brothers almost right away. We aged out together, and I wanted him to join the army with me, but he wasn't interested. Yet, although we took different paths in life, we were still family, always in touch. He was the only person I trusted completely, the only person I had a real bond with. Of course I blame myself for not considering what the pain medication might do to him."

She'd been holding onto his shirt the entire time, but now she wrapped her arms around his waist and hugged him as tightly as he'd been hugging her.

"You can't keep blaming yourself, Cort. There was nothing you could do."

He leaned back, and used the side of his hand to lift her chin, so they were eye to eye.

"I'll stop, if you will."

As she looked into Cort's dark, pain-filled gaze, Liz's heart skipped one beat, then another, before it began to race. The emotions battering her were as overwhelming as they were unexpected, making her eyes sting with tears all over again. Yet she couldn't put name to them. They were alien, unrecognizable. She should be frightened by them but she wasn't.

Being held so tightly in his arms had muted her sorrow to melancholy, and it felt right to agree to let her guilt over Andrew go, although she knew doing so wouldn't be easy. She'd carried it too long, let it become ingrained over the years. But if saying she was willing to let it go would ease the pain Cort carried...

"I'll stop," she whispered, searching his face, feeling a weight lift from her chest when his lips quirked upward. "Will you?"

"I know I have to. It hurts too much to keep thinking that way." He took a deep breath, sighing on the exhalation. "And Brody wouldn't like knowing I'm twisting myself up in knots over him. He was too down to earth for that."

Before she could reply, there was the distant clatter of helicopter blades, bringing Liz suddenly back to reality. She blinked, almost surprised to realize they were still on the roof. It felt as though she'd fallen through the rabbit hole and landed in a new, unexplored country.

She stepped back, breaking their embrace, glancing around. They were alone in the dusk beneath the still overcast sky, the noise of the city muted. Her heart felt light and yet beat with deep, steady ferocity.

All she wanted was to be back in his arms, to hear his voice in her ear, sink into the warmth of his strong embrace. A little voice in the back of her head whispered she was over-emotional, needed to gather her self-containment around her once more, so as to stave off the danger.

But she didn't listen.

"I want to hear more about him," she heard herself say, as if from a distance. "Come home with me."

For all the time they'd spent together, she'd never invited him to her home, needing that last little bit of distance, a sanctuary. Now there was nowhere she'd rather be, and no one she'd rather be there with.

Cort's gaze scoured her face for what seemed an eternity until he said, "I'd like that."

After changing into their street clothing, they caught a cab to her townhome, and she led him up the steps to her door. Suddenly clumsy, she fumbled her keys, almost dropping them, before fitting the correct one into the lock.

They stepped inside into the darkened hall, lit only by a small nightlight she kept burning for those times she came in late.

As she reached for the light switch, his hand caught hers and he pulled her back into his arms.

No words now, just the hot, hard pressure of his lips on hers, the almost frantic embrace. Hands finding fastenings, sweeping over flesh, holding on, pulling closer.

For a moment it was like being swept back in time to Mexico, when the power of their attraction had been purely carnal, and there had been no barriers between them.

No need to hide, to protect herself against him, since she'd been sure she'd never see him again.

The first night he had taken her with such concentrated passion she'd been forced to run the next morning, unwilling, perhaps even unable to face him in the morning light.

Now, though, she knew him, had every reason in the world to pull up the drawbridge and secure her emotions in the stone castle of her heart.

But it was impossible to do that tonight.

Her resistance had melted away as he'd held her on the roof, as though trying to shelter her from pain. Everyone always assumed she was capable of handling anything and everything life threw at her. It had been that way all her life, with her family, Andrew, even her friends. They assumed the cool, tough façade she wore went right down to her soul, so rarely did anyone ask if she was okay, if she needed them, their strength or understanding.

Cort hadn't just asked, he'd given it freely, and turned her heart upside down at the same time.

Now she knew she'd never be able to close him out completely again and, instead of being terrified, she was elated. A strange new power seemed to flow through her blood and bones and sinews.

She wanted Cort, more than she'd ever wanted him before.

"Liz," he growled, as she pushed his shirt off over his head. "Which way?"

Without a word, she led him into her living room, turning on a lamp as she went.

"Sit." She pointed to the couch.

Cort sank down onto it as ordered, and held out one hand.

"Join me."

"Shush," she said, standing in front of him, imbued with the need to make him as crazy as he always made her. "In a minute."

He'd always taken the lead in their lovemaking, and she'd enjoyed every moment of it, but tonight felt different. Cort had cracked her emotions open like a clamshell, and she wanted to pour them out all over him. That wasn't part of their bargain, though, so the physical fulfillment of that need would have to suffice.

She undressed slowly, revealing her body to him, watching as his eyes darkened to gleaming black. As she took off each article of clothing she remembered how he'd touched her, making her feel beautiful with the purposeful movement of his fingers, the sweep of his palm, the forceful-ness of his embrace. His strength matched and complemented her own, so she never felt over-powered, simply feminine as he urged her to new heights of desire and ecstasy.

As the last article of clothing fell, she trembled, almost unbearably aroused by the expression of need tightening his face, the way his eyes burned as they moved with delicious intent across her body.

He held out his hands to her, but she shook her head, taking a step forward to kneel between his thighs. She was surprised to realize her fingers were steady as she reached for the button on his waistband.

"Wait," she said. "Let me…"

The rasp of his zipper going down was loud in the room, where the only other sounds were their breathing. He shifted to help her pull his pants and underwear down and off, and then he settled against the back of the couch once more.

"Now?" he asked, his voice little more than a growl.

"Almost," she replied, as she put his clothing aside.

He obviously wasn't prepared for the swipe of her tongue along the length of his erection, if the hiss of his breath was any indication. The sound of Cort groaning her name pushed her own desire even higher, but she didn't relent in the attention she lavished on him. Beneath her fingers his powerful thigh muscles tensed, coiling tight, yet the hand he placed on her head was gentle, not insistent.

"Liz." The rasp of his voice was like music to her ears. "Babe, please."

She'd taken him to the edge, and now she eased him down tenderly, letting him catch his breath for a moment. Lifting her head, she found him looking down at her, his eyes barely open, his face flushed and damp.

With a little moan of surrender she rose to straddle him, taking him deep, shuddering at the way he filled her completely. Body. Mind. Soul.

It was sublime, with a bitter-sweet edge that made it even more precious and arousing.

Rising and falling, slowly rocking, she took them both back to the edge, then her movements becoming frantic, demanding.

"Wait," he gasped.

But she didn't listen. She knew he'd reached the end of his control, and reveled in the knowing.

Then he slipped his hand between their bodies, and touched her in just the right way.

And they flew.

CHAPTER THIRTEEN

CORT SAT AT the table, watching Liz as she moved with her usual calm efficiency around the kitchen, putting together a snack for them to share. Music played in the background, and she hummed along. Neither of them seemed inclined to speak, and that suited Cort fine just then.

Something had changed between them. He felt it, like embers in the air, stinging his skin, making it hard to breathe. Liz didn't seem affected, her demeanor unaltered.

So the change must be in him.

Memories of their lovemaking filled his head like smoke. Although satiated, his body stirred anew thinking about the way she'd made love to him, taking control, making him lose his. In a strange way he felt it as another form of her surrender, the power of it entering his bones, pushing him across an emotional line from which there was no return.

Goose bumps rose on his arms and along his

spine, and he forced those thoughts away, unwilling, unable to face them just then.

Theirs was not a traditional relationship. The boundaries had been firmly established. Neither of them was looking for any kind of commitment, and he would be moving on in a few short months. He hoped that when he did, the friendship they'd developed would endure. Perhaps there'd be visits, as he passed through New York on his way somewhere else, birthday and Christmas cards, telephone conversations in between. That was the best-case scenario, in his mind, so why did thinking that way make him feel melancholy, as though the end was about to come tonight?

To distract himself, Cort looked around the huge kitchen, his gaze settling on a photograph on the mantelpiece above the fireplace. It was of a young, blond man, smiling into the camera as though he were the master of all that lay before him. Was that the man who had broken Liz's heart, who'd left her unwilling to trust, to believe in love again?

"That's my brother, Robbie." There was no mistaking the fondness in her voice. "He was about twenty-one when that was taken. He was always such a party animal, it still seems surreal to think about him getting married."

She'd talked about the upcoming wedding, and he'd heard the ambivalence in her voice, but hadn't pried. Before today she'd been so private, hoarding personal information like a dragon with its gold, so her family situation was still a mystery to him.

Now somehow it seemed okay to ask, "Do you like his fiancée?"

"I do. She's been good for him. You'd think, with him being in finance and Giovanna a fashion model, he'd be the more grounded, but it's the opposite way around."

Turning from the chopping block, where she was cutting cheese into squares, she gave him one of her penetrating looks.

"Did I ever tell you that Robbie was adopted?"

Surprised and intrigued, he replied, "No, you didn't."

"I was about five and he was two when he came to live with us and, to me, it was as though he belonged as much as, if not more than, I did. I can safely say he's my best friend, and was from that first day we met."

Cort was glad she'd turned back to her chore,

not looking at his face. Hearing her say how much she loved her brother caused him a totally unreasonable flash of jealousy, which he was sure showed in his expression before he got it under control.

It must be the stress of the day, making him react that way.

"Here's the thing," she continued. "A few years ago Robbie meets Giovanna, and he falls like a rock. He chases her all over the world, wherever she's modeling, until she agrees to marry him. Then he goes to my parents and finally asks about his birth parents."

"He hadn't before?"

She shook her head.

"You'd have to know Robbie, and my parents, to understand why it took that long. My parents don't talk about feelings, about emotion, or any part of the past that isn't perfectly respectable. It's ill bred, *common*."

The emphasis she put on the word actually made him smile. She'd sounded like an old schoolteacher.

"And Robbie…well…he's the complete opposite of me, really. He's friendly, charming, outgoing, smiles all the time. He doesn't like to rock the boat, wants everyone to be happy."

The knife in her hand stilled for a moment then she shrugged lightly.

"I think he just figured if they'd wanted to tell him, they would have. Anyway, he finally asks about his parents, and it turns out he's actually my father's child. The product of an affair Dad had not long after my mother had me."

He hadn't seen that one coming, and felt his eyebrows go up.

She gave him a sideways look over her shoulder. "Right? So, you see, I'm still a little…upset with my father. What kind of man has an affair when his wife just had a baby?"

Cort was still trying to process what she'd told him. "And your mom knew your brother was actually your father's child?"

"Yes. Isn't that insane? I wish I could understand how it all came about. It's really eaten at me since I heard, and I haven't really spoken to my father since."

"I know you said your parents don't talk about things, but can't you ask them?"

Her sigh almost broke his heart.

"I know it won't make a difference. My mom

looked so frightened when she talked about it, and Dad just walked away. They haven't even told Robbie the full story, only that when his birth mother got sick and was dying, my mom agreed to take him in. Honestly, she's treated him as though he were her own, without any reservations. They're actually closer than my mom and I are."

That gave him pause, as he worked it all through in his head.

Why was she so angry at her father for something that had happened so long ago? It hadn't destroyed her family. In fact, she'd ended up with a sibling she obviously adored. Remembering how upset Liz had been with the young stabbing victim who was still worried about the man who'd almost killed her, he had to ask.

"You're not angry with your mother?"

Laying down the knife, she busied herself with arranging everything on a platter.

"I always thought of my mom as being delicate, you know? I couldn't be the daughter she wanted, so I try not to hurt her any more than I have to, and my being angry with her would hurt her horribly."

When he was young he'd longed for a family,

believing it would be like in the TV shows. Of course, as he'd grown older he'd realized relationships weren't as simple as portrayed in the media, but the complexity of Liz's family made his head swim a little.

One thing was obvious, though. Liz somehow saw herself as a disappointment to her mother, which seemed crazy to Cort. What mother wouldn't love to have a beautiful, successful woman like Liz as their child? He also wondered if Liz saw her mother's actions in forgiving her husband and accepting his child into her family as a weakness. It made sense, considering Liz's overall view of love.

"I think," he said slowly, "your mother is probably a lot stronger than you give her credit for. I mean, she has to be, to have forgiven your father and treated your brother the way she has. Why not ask her, let her explain what happened? At least then you can maybe put it behind you."

Still with her back to him, Liz muttered, "It wouldn't be an easy conversation to have."

"I'm sure it won't be, especially since you say talking things through isn't your family's way, but it might be the best thing. For you, at any rate."

Which was all he really cared about anyway.

Finally she turned and walked over to the table, carrying the platter, her noncommittal expression one he knew well.

"Let's eat," was all she said.

Everything had changed, but Liz was determined not to let Cort see. As usual busying herself, being useful, allowed her to avoid revealing her emotional state, which was frankly chaotic.

The entire day had taken its toll on her, but she didn't regret any of it, just didn't want to think too deeply about what was happening to her feelings for Cort right now.

Better to do that when she was alone.

In the meantime, talking about Robbie and her family helped to take the edge off. Cort had a way of cutting through to the heart of things, she mused as they munched their way through the platter of cold cuts, antipasto, vegetables, cheeses and crusty bread.

While she'd been concentrating on being angry with her father, it was just a way to avoid acknowledging it was her mother she really needed to speak to.

It all just seemed so complicated, and she

sometimes found herself wishing Robbie had never asked about his origins. Yet she could completely understand his need to know, and felt selfish whenever she had those thoughts.

"Have you ever tried to find your parents?"

She saw Cort stiffen, and then his shoulders relaxed fractionally, and he shook his head.

"No, I haven't."

"Never wanted to?"

"When we were younger, Brody and I used to talk about it, trying to decide whether to do it or not. In his case, he'd lived with his mother until she died, when he was eight. His father was never in the picture, and he figured it was probably for the best. Who knew what he'd dig up, trying to find out? In my case, I couldn't see the upside to finding the people who tossed me out with the trash, you know?"

As nonchalant as he tried to sound, she heard the residual pain in his voice. Who could blame him? She'd guess it was something he'd had to reconcile himself to, even if it had been the most hurtful thing anyone could do.

"I understand, but you're stronger than I am. My curiosity would have gotten the best of me."

"In one respect I gave in to my curiosity. I got

my DNA tested, for medical purposes, a couple years ago. Well, that and because I was tired of people asking me what my ancestry was." He smiled slightly. "People would ask me if I'm Hispanic, Brazilian, Native American, Italian. Hell, when I was in the army there was a Filipino guy who could have been my brother. And, before you ask, no, he actually *wasn't* my brother. I checked."

Filipino, Italian, Native American, Hispanic. Yes, she could see him fitting into any of those groups.

"So, what was the result?"

"I'm almost exactly one half Native American and one half European, mostly Irish."

"Exactly half?" That was strange.

"Yep, pretty much."

She turned over all she knew about DNA testing in her head. "It's a shame it can't pinpoint a tribe, isn't it?"

Cort shrugged, but she read tension in the set of his shoulders. "Not really. It's not that important."

"Hmm. I asked Robbie what had prompted him to want to find out about his birth parents, and he just said, "Everybody wants to know where they

come from so they can figure out where to go."
Pretty profound, for my knucklehead brother,
but it made sense to me."

Cort swallowed the last of his bread smeared
with Brie before he replied.

"Everybody needs something different in life,
I guess."

Like she needed the stability of Hepplewhite
and New York City, and he need the adventure
of traveling around.

"True," she replied, trying to ignore the ache
in her chest at that admission.

"So, are you going to talk to your mom about
what happened?"

"Maybe after the wedding. Everything is too
crazy right now." She was prevaricating, and
even she realized it.

Cort gave her a sympathetic smile. "You'd
probably enjoy the wedding more if you got past
it, though. Nothing like unspoken tension to ruin
a happy occasion."

He was right, of course, but she knew she
wouldn't.

"There's too much going on, getting ready
for the wedding. Mom's already in a tailspin.

Throwing that at her right now would be down-right unkind."

She ruminated on her own cowardice for a moment, but then an idea hit her, and made her heart race.

For too long she'd run from emotions, feelings, happiness. Lied to herself that she didn't need anyone. Today had, if nothing else, shown how good it could be to have someone to lean on, even if just for a little while.

Until Cort left New York, or decided to end their affair, he was hers, and she didn't want to deny herself the pleasure of being with him. While others made her doubt herself, something about him made her feel stronger than she ever had before. She would take advantage of that for as long as she could.

"What?" Cort asked, the corners of his lips lifting.

"You know what would make my mother very, very happy? If you came to the wedding with me."

"What?" he asked again, this time with a tone of such horror it actually made her snicker.

"She's asked me a million times if I'm bringing anyone, and it would be a huge favor to me if you'd come."

"But—"

"Cort, listen. We both know you'll be gone on to your next adventure in a few months, and this thing between us will be over, but my mom doesn't know that. It'll make her happy to think I'm in a relationship, you'll have a great time, and it might even pave the way to my having that difficult conversation with her."

The last part she threw in for effect, knowing nothing would make that talk any easier, but also cognizant of Cort's belief in the importance of it. Manipulative? Maybe a little. But having Cort around would make the wedding more bearable.

She really was dreading it.

"First off, isn't it dishonest to let your mother think our relationship is more than it really is? And, secondly, I'm pretty sure I wouldn't fit in with your family and their friends."

"Yes, and no," she answered succinctly. "It is sort of dishonest, but you have no idea how much pressure I feel every time she asks me about my relationship status. It would get her off my back, at least for a little while, and genuinely make her happy. I don't see the problem with that, as long as we're on the same page.

"As for you not fitting in, besides the fact that Robbie and Giovanna have a wide variety of friends, and my family, both sides of it, are a mess, you're a handsome, charming doctor with a sterling reputation. Believe me, you'll fit in better than I will."

The look he gave her made her feel twitchy. It was the kind of expression that said, louder than words, that he saw through her argument to the heart of the matter once more.

And her instincts were proven correct when he said, "You really aren't sure of your place in your family, are you?"

How could she explain it to him when it was something she'd grappled with all her life? But she felt as though she owed it to him to at least try.

"I know they love me," she said slowly, "but I've really never felt as if I fit in. They're charming and sociable and, in their own way, affectionate. I've always felt a little distant, never knew how to get along in the world they traverse so easily, and always knew I wasn't able to meet my parents' expectations. So I set my own, and decided to live my own life, and that just widened the gap."

Without warning, he reached across the table and took her hand, rubbing his thumb over her knuckles, the smile on his face both gentle and conspiratorial.

"Can I say, from my perspective, it's a life well lived? I'm so glad we met, because you've opened up my horizons in the best of ways. I think you're amazing, and shame on your parents if they don't too."

Warmth flared up into her face. Dear goodness, when was the last time she'd blushed? Maybe fourth grade? It made her want to duck her head, but Cort held her gaze with his effortlessly. Best to capitalize on the moment, if she could.

"So you'll come with me?"

His lips quirked, and although he shook his head he also said, "Yes."

CHAPTER FOURTEEN

BEFORE LIZ COULD even touch him, the patient jerked away.

"Whaddaya doing? Haven't yah poked me enough?"

As his alcohol-soaked breath blew across her face, Liz tried not to inhale too much of it. While he'd been given thiamine and glucose intravenously, and had been in the ER for a while, he was still intoxicated enough for some symptoms to potentially be masked. Frequent examinations were necessary to make sure nothing had been missed, although she suspected the old saw about drunks and children being protected was true of this patient. His injuries were minor, considering he'd been struck by a car.

"Mr. Kendrick, I have to keep checking you to make sure you don't have internal injuries."

"But I'm fine."

As if to prove it he tried to roll, perhaps to sit

up, but was stopped by both Liz and the attending nurse holding him down.

"I'm afraid that isn't true. You were hit by a car. At the very least you have a broken nose and I suspect a fractured ankle."

"Jush get thish thing off me and let me go home. I tell you, I'm fine."

Liz and the nurse, Marta, then found themselves in a bit of a wrestling match with the inebriated patient over the cervical collar. Although Liz hadn't detected any neck or back injuries, she wasn't taking any chances and had ordered a C-spine X-ray, which hadn't been done yet. Just as Mr. Kendrick gave up, apparently deciding instead to treat them to a mangled, off-key rendition of a song Liz was sure she'd never heard before, the door opened and Cort walked in.

For a moment even Mr. Kendrick went still, and Liz's knees went ridiculously weak on seeing him, her entire body thrumming to life.

She refused to think about how attached she was getting to Cort. How he'd invaded every facet of her life. A part of her wanted to just enjoy it all, but the realist in her kept reminding her that he wasn't going to stick around so she should start rebuilding her defenses.

That was proving extremely difficult.

Which was why she made sure to keep her work persona intact with him.

But it didn't help that just seeing him filled her with warmth and still made her sometimes forget what she was doing.

Like just now.

Gathering herself, she asked, "Can I help you?"

The words came out sharper than she'd planned, but Cort didn't seem fazed.

"I was called down to examine an accident victim. I could have sworn this was the room they told me to come to."

"Oh, no." There was clear annoyance in Marta's voice. "We have a trainee on the desk today, and she's been messing things up terribly. I know I told her Dr. Nolan Smith, the orthopedic surgeon. I'll go and rectify the situation, Dr. Prudhomme."

She made a beeline for the door, and Liz replied, "Thank you, Marta."

"Doc. Doc!" Mr. Kendrick lifted a hand and waved it at Cort. "Can you get these women off me, please? I just wanna go home and they won't let me."

Cort stepped closer to the bed, into a position where Mr. Kendrick could see him clearly, thankfully on the opposite side from Liz. She'd had to attend Giovanna's bridal shower, which had been a two-day spa retreat in the Hamptons. While she'd enjoyed the change of scenery and the pampering, the downside had been two nights away from Cort, and she was feeling the lack. The last thing she needed right now was to be too close to him. She might forget herself and touch him.

Her fingers tingled at the thought.

"Well, if they won't let you, it's because they have good reason. Why don't you just relax and let Dr. Prudhomme fix you up?"

"There's nothing to fix. I feel great."

Cort shook his head. "Listen, Dr. Prudhomme is one of the best. Let her take care of you, and you'll be out of here as soon as possible."

Mr. Kendrick replied with a belch, then mumbled under his breath. Cort shot Liz a knowing half smile, then said, "Sorry for the intrusion. I'll be on my way."

Before she realized what he was about to do, Mr. Kendrick grabbed Liz's wrist, saying, "My face hurts. And my leg."

The drip was finally doing its job, sobering

him up enough for the pain to break through. "I'm sure they do, Mr. Kendrick. As I told you, you have a broken nose and an ankle injury. Does anywhere else hurt?"

"No. No," he mumbled, closing his eyes. "I don't think so."

But something bothered her about the bruising she'd noticed as they'd cut away his clothing. Still, she hesitated. If she let Cort leave and then called for a surgeon, someone else might respond and she wouldn't have to deal with working with him right now.

Realizing what she was doing, she gave herself a mental kick in the butt. Endangering a patient because her hormones were in disarray? Ridiculous.

"Excuse me, Dr. Smith," she called out, just as Cort got to the door. "A moment, please?"

As it turned out, Mr. Kendrick had a splenic rupture requiring surgery.

After Cort left to go and scrub in, while Liz was signing off on her part of Mr. Kendrick's care, she was still brooding about her almost compulsive need to be around Cort, which led her to think about the days just past.

The spa retreat hadn't been all fun for her. Giovanna, caught up in what Liz thought of as "bride fever," had turned her attention to Liz.

"We need to find you a good man," she'd declared to the entire group at dinner. "I don't understand why no one has snapped you up yet."

Thankfully, Giovanna hadn't mentioned Liz was bringing a plus one to the wedding. Probably because Liz had explained Cort was just a friend from work, invited to get Lorelei off her back about her constantly single state. Giovanna had bought the story without question.

Liz's cousin, Moira, had giggled and interjected, "I'm not sure the man exists who could deal with Liz. He'd either have to be a saint or a doormat."

"What do you mean by that?" Giovanna asked, obviously annoyed and narrowing her eyes at the other woman.

But Moira just shrugged. "Liz is stubborn, and cranky. Not to mention obsessed with her job. What man's going to put up with that long term? He'd have to either deal with constant arguing or give in all the time."

"She's none of those things!"

Liz loved the way Giovanna had jumped to her

defense, but she was forced to admit, "I am dedicated to my job. And stubborn too." She drew the line at admitting to "cranky," although all her life she'd had people constantly telling her to smile, and getting annoyed when she refused. If that made her cranky, so be it.

"And you're difficult," Moira pointed out, obviously enjoying herself. "Everyone says so."

Unable to resist, Liz gave her cousin a bland look, and rebutted, "People only say that when I won't give in to them, and they know I'm right. Who has time to pander to anyone's ego like that?"

"*If* you were married, or even seriously involved with someone, you'd *have* to, just for a peaceful life," said another woman.

That started a debate about the fragility of the male ego, and the lengths women sometimes had to go to in order to get their own way. Sitting back and listening to it, Liz knew herself incapable of sustaining a relationship if that was what it took. Yet she didn't feel superior, or disdainful toward the other women, just pensive and a little sad, as it seemed to solidify all the thoughts she'd had about herself.

She also couldn't help wondering if this type

of mind-set was what had led her mother to forgive her husband and take in his love child to raise as her own. Yet wouldn't there be some of the thinly veiled resentment the women she was listening to confessed to feeling and acting out in myriad little ways? Lorelei Prudhomme had never exhibited that, as far as Liz could see. And if she'd done so to her husband, would that bond, that united front they always exhibited as a couple, truly exist?

The more she wondered about it, the more confused she got. Cort had said she'd need to get to the bottom of it before she could get past it, and he was probably right. But the more time that passed, the more it seemed she was the only one who wanted to know, and the harder it became to bring up. While she was direct and no-nonsense with everyone else in her life, somehow it was almost impossible to be that way with her parents.

Old habits ran too deep.

Now, as the nurses were wheeling Mr. Kendrick up to the surgical floor, Liz's phone vibrated, and her heart missed a beat when she realized it was Cort texting.

You busy tonight?

No.

Thankfully, Robbie's friend Simon had taken on the stag party organization, and since it was being held at an exclusive, men's only club, Liz not only didn't have to go but was actively *not* invited.

Meet me at my apartment after work? Got my uniform back from the cleaners. You need to tell me if it still fits.

Sure.

Looking at her laconic reply and comparing it with the eagerness she actually felt at the thought of being with Cort that evening made her snort. Just the thought of him in his uniform made her mouth water.

He'd be lucky if he got a word out before she jumped all over him. As much as she hated to admit it, even to herself, she'd missed him that much.

The city had been struck by a rare mid-June heatwave, catching many people by surprise. Apparently including the maintenance people at Cort's apartment building, which he realized when he got home that evening to find the air-conditioners weren't working.

Letting himself into the apartment, he found Liz lying on the couch with a couple of fans blowing directly on her. All she was wearing were her panties and a thin cotton camisole, sweat making them stick to her luscious curves, revealing more than they concealed.

"Why didn't you call and tell me what was going on here?" he asked, closing the door behind him, wanting only to go over there and make her even sweatier. "We could have met at your place instead."

"I don't mind," she replied, stretching one leg out and pointing her toes at him. The motion was erotic, electrifying his blood, making him instantly hard. "I like the heat. Makes a nice change from the winter and cold, damp spring. Hopefully it'll go away before the wedding, though, or I'll be a sweltering mess."

He dropped his backpack and toed off his shoes, his eyes never leaving her. They knew each other well enough now to know the signals. Liz wasn't in the mood to talk and, truth be told, neither was Cort.

It had only been a couple of days that she'd

been gone, two nights when he'd tossed and turned and woken up in the morning, disappointed not to have her draped across his chest. The sense of danger rising inside him ever since that day on the hospital roof had grown almost too insistent for him to ignore, but once more he pushed it aside. There was no way he could ignore his visceral attraction to her as he watched her eyelids slide almost closed, saw her lick her lips in anticipation.

He unbuttoned his shirt. Once it was off, he made short work of the rest of his clothes. Liz shifted on the couch, her fingers curling into her palms.

She was waiting for him to take control, and the sense of power her quiescence gave him sent a streak of fire through his blood. He could never get enough of that feeling. Never get enough of her.

The thought made his heart miss a beat, but it didn't make his hunger for her abate, his ravenous desire, his heart-deep want.

Later he'd deal with the fallout, plan his exit strategy, before it became impossible to contemplate. Before he made a fool of himself and opened the way to the heartbreak he knew this glorious woman would cause.

Right now, though, all he could see, all he could think about was her.

CHAPTER FIFTEEN

THE DAY OF the wedding dawned bright and warm, the heatwave thankfully having dissipated. Cort took a last look at himself in the mirror before leaving the house, making sure his mess uniform was pristine.

It felt strange to have it on again after all this time. He'd contemplated renting a suit for the wedding but had decided not to. He wasn't going to go to Liz's brother's wedding as anyone or anything other than himself. While being an army medical officer no longer defined him, it was still better than pretending he was the kind of man who had a morning suit hanging in his closet, no doubt perfectly pressed by his valet.

Did men even have valets anymore? And if they did, did those valets press their suits?

Those were the kinds of questions Liz, and most of the people he was about to meet, would have answers to, whereas Cort had no clue.

Weird, the types of things that went through

his mind when he was on edge. And he definitely was on edge. He'd go so far as to say nervous, which wasn't a sensation he enjoyed in the slightest. Neither he nor Liz had been at their best the last few days. Cort had tried to put it down to the fact the hospital had problems with some of the new equipment and staff, making normal activities more difficult than usual. And, of course, there was the upcoming wedding, which necessitated her running up and down and them spending less time together.

But he knew there was more to it than that, at least on his part. He couldn't shake the feeling this wedding was going to prove the beginning of the end for his intimate relationship with Liz. He didn't believe in precognition or anything like that, but had felt something building between them, like the precursor to lightning. Or a harbinger of a turning point, and he had no reason to believe it would be a positive one. Cort did believe in following his instincts, and those instincts were telling him to brace for whatever was coming.

Better yet, get out in front of it, which was what he'd been trying to do. He always felt better with a plan B in his back pocket.

Cort just didn't want to think about telling Liz his plans. Not that she'd care one way or the other. But he cared. Thinking about saying good-bye to her made him feel slightly nauseous.

Not the time to think about it, he told himself, checking his appearance one last time then brushing at a barely visible speck of dust on his service cap. Getting through the day was going to be stressful enough.

Right on time, the car service called to say the town car was downstairs, and Cort let himself out of the apartment.

"Don't worry about it," Liz had said yesterday, before heading off to the hotel where all the wedding party was staying. "I told Giovanna and Robbie you were just a friend I invited to keep Mom off my back and neither Mom nor Dad are the kind to question you about our relationship. Although Mom will make a fuss over you, wanting to make a good impression, in case you stick around."

She'd said the last part with a small chuckle, acknowledging the fact they both knew that wasn't going to happen.

Neither telling himself he, in turn, didn't need to make a good impression, nor reminding himself he'd faced far more dangerous missions, helped. Whatever the relationship really was between Liz and her family, the last thing Cort wanted was to do anything to make it worse. And he couldn't see an upside to her fooling her parents about her relationship status. If it came out later, wouldn't they be hurt by the subterfuge?

However it all fell out, he'd decided to make the most of the time they had together, if Liz would let him. Sometime, in the not-too-distant future, it would all be over and he wanted as many memories of her as he could make.

About a block and a half before they got to the church, they hit a traffic jam. Ahead Cort could see barricades across the road, and was about to ask the driver if there was a problem when she said, "It'll take a little while to get to the church, sir, but we're in good time. You won't be late."

To his surprise, he realized not only was the road barricaded so the wedding guests could be dropped off at the entrance to the church but there were photographers and videographers outside.

"The paparazzi are out in full force," the driver remarked cheerfully while they waited their turn to get to the head of the line, as though that were the most normal thing in the world. "Everyone wants to see Giovanna Alberghetti's wedding dress."

Cort hadn't even known who Giovanna was until Liz had mentioned her brother was marrying the woman. He'd come into the situation already feeling completely out of his depth, and it wasn't getting any better.

Thankfully, none of the photographers were interested in him when he got out of car. It was a relief to walk up the steps of the cathedral without any of the excitement he'd witnessed after the car ahead had disgorged its passengers, who, according to his driver, were a couple of fashion models and their sports star husbands.

In the narthex he joined the line of people snaking into the church, and when Cort gave his name to an usher at the door the young man smiled.

"Oh, yes, Major Smith. This way, please."

They proceeded up the main aisle, Cort expecting to be slotted into one of the back pews, but once they passed the halfway mark and kept going, his stomach dropped down into his socks. Aware of people turning to look at him, no doubt wondering who this nobody was, he kept his eyes straight ahead and pretended to be on military parade.

"Here we are, Major."

The usher stood back and gestured Cort into the second row on the right of the aisle.

A pew even he knew was usually reserved for family.

There were already a few elderly couples seated at the opposite end of the row, and one of the gentlemen gave Cort a very obvious once-over before nodding at him then turning to face forward again.

Gathering himself, not wanting to make a scene, Cort said, "Thank you," and stepped into the pew.

He was quite sure there'd been a mistake, and dreaded the embarrassment of someone coming to move him farther back in the church. In the meantime, however, all he could do was pretend it was all fine.

There wasn't much space left in the pew, so he moved down as far as he could go without crowding the lady he was next to, and sat down, balancing his cover on his knees.

It was tempting to simply stare straight ahead,

but a glance to his right found the lady next to him smiling his way, so he returned the gesture. That was all she needed.

Leaning toward him, she whispered, "Who are you, young man?"

"Dr. Cort Smith, ma'am," he replied just as softly.

"I'm Melisande Prudhomme, the groom's great-aunt. Are you Eliza's young man? I heard she had someone accompanying her today, but wasn't sure I believed it."

In for a penny, in for a pound.

"Yes, ma'am, I am accompanying Liz."

Her face brightened. "I'm so glad to see her with someone, and someone of substance too. Are you stationed nearby, or are you two having one of those long-distance relationships?" She waggled a finger at him. "Those hardly ever work, you know."

"I'm retired from the military, ma'am. Liz and I work together."

"Oh, that's better, then. And you should call me Aunt Millie, like Eliza does."

The gentleman seated beside Melisande leaned forward and said, "Stop interrogating the major,

Millie." Then he stuck out his hand toward Cort. "Cecil Prudhomme. This busybody's husband."

Cort suppressed a grin, as he shook the proffered hand. "Dr. Cort Smith. It's a pleasure to meet you, sir."

"I'd introduce you to the rest of the folks in the pew, but it might cause a bit of a commotion. My sister, Bunny, is as deaf as a post and given to bellowing rather than speaking. Whispering is far beyond her capabilities at this point. You'll meet them all at the reception."

"Bunny's also a little gaga," Aunt Millie whispered, a mischievous twinkle in her eye. "If she asks you what you did in the war, just be warned she'll be talking about World War Two."

"Millie. Behave," Cecil Prudhomme said, but there was undeniable amusement in his voice.

"Thank you for the head's up, ma'am," Cort replied, unable to suppress a little chuckle.

The organ, which had been playing classical music quietly in the background, suddenly took on a more sonorous tone, and a ripple of excitement ran through the congregation.

A door to the right of the altar opened and a man Cort recognized as Liz's brother Robbie stepped through, followed closely by Liz.

But this was a Liz Cort had never seen before. Sophisticated.

Movie-star glamorous.

Gloriously encased in a dress that, although it mimicked her brother's suit in coloring, showcased her beauty in such a way that Cort was left wondering who would bother to look at the bride.

Creamy shoulders rose from a low-cut neckline, framed by a wide, dark gray collar. The buff-colored bodice somehow wrapped and emphasized Liz's perfect, curvy body, while the same gray came around to cinch her waist and fall away almost like the tails of the men's morning suits. Beneath was revealed a straight skirt, seemingly of the same fabric as her brother's trousers.

She was so beautiful he couldn't take his eyes off her and his heart skipped a beat as heat gathered at the base of his spine.

Liz scanned the front rows, and her gaze settled on him. She didn't smile, but the corners of her lips twitched and she sent him a little wink, before walking to her place at her brother's side.

"Oh, how lovely Eliza looks," Aunt Millie sighed, while giving Cort a surprisingly hearty poke in the side. "If that dress doesn't give you naughty ideas, young man, I'll be sadly disappointed in you."

"Oh, it does, ma'am," he whispered back.

At the same time her husband said, "Millie!"

The wedding service went off without a hitch. Even Giovanna was on time, for what was probably the first time ever, Robbie whispered to Liz with a chuckle. Testament, Liz thought, to her now sister-in-law's delight in marrying the man she'd so assiduously fended off for almost a year.

Of course, after the ceremony the wedding party and immediate family had to have pictures taken, and by the time they got close to the end of the photo shoot Liz was impatient.

She was worried about Cort. How he was managing by himself at the prereception gathering. Mind you, he'd been sitting next to her Aunt Millie in the church, and if there was anyone who'd be inclined to take him under their wing, it was her.

She really shouldn't have been concerned. As the wedding party made their entrance into the beautifully decorated ballroom where the wedding brunch was being held, she spotted Cort standing to one side, sandwiched between Aunt Millie and Aunt Bunny.

"Good grief," she muttered, earning a laughing look from Robbie as he followed her gaze and saw the trio.

"Your poor guy," Robbie said.

"He's not—"

"Your guy," her brother finished for her. "So you've said ad nauseam."

Liz sent him a glower, which just made him laugh. It was a continuation of sorts of their conversation in the church.

"That guy of yours looks like he's contemplating how to get that dress off you." Robbie smirked, apparently unbearably pleased with himself and wanting to spread the love around. "And don't bother to tell me you're just friends. I know you too well, you know."

She hadn't even realized she'd gone back to staring at Cort, so handsome in his dress blues, until her brother's comment hit home.

"Buzz off," she'd replied out of the corner of her mouth, as their mother appeared at the end of the aisle on the arm of an usher, their father walking behind them.

Watching her parents coming toward them,

beaming with pride, caused a flood of emotion so intense it was as though a hand closed around her heart. Instinctively she looked again at Cort, seeking reassurance, and when he smiled at her she was suddenly able to breathe again.

"Will you at least talk to Dad today?" Robbie had asked. "Rather than pretend to?"

That question still echoed in her head hours later, and she still hadn't formulated an answer. Her father and her had drifted around each other like planets whose orbits never really crossed, although Liz thought she'd seen a hint of melancholy in Brant's gaze when she'd caught him looking at her.

What she needed to say to her father, to ask him, wasn't an appropriate subject for such a happy day, was it? Even as she justified her continued silence, she knew herself to be a coward.

It was really her mother she needed to break the silence. To, in a strange way, give Liz permission to forgive her father. In her heart, Liz already knew how sorry Brant was, but the anger she felt on her mother's behalf kept her holding him at arm's length.

Giovanna had planned a simple yet elegant brunch for after the ceremony, but the real party wasn't until the evening. In between she and Robbie would have some more pictures taken and then supposedly rest up for the festivities to come. The ravenous way her brother looked at his gorgeous bride made Liz think he had something other than resting on his mind for those hours in between.

"You look amazing," Cort said softly, for her ears only, as he held out her chair for her. Thankfully Giovanna had dispensed with a more formal seating plan and they were sitting together. "That dress wraps you up like the perfect present."

She gave him a bland look as he waited for the other ladies to be seated, standing beside her with his hand on the back of her chair, his fingers just brushing the exposed skin of her shoulder.

"You like gifts, don't you?" she asked, earning herself a heavy-lidded look that turned her insides liquid with desire.

"So, who are you?" Moira asked, giving Cort a flirtatious look as she slid into her chair, despite her husband being right there.

Straight-faced, Liz answered. "Oh, this is Saint Cort Smith. Cort, my cousin Moira."

Moira turned pink and, after a hasty greeting,

quickly turned to speak to Giovanna's cousin, who was seated next to her. The men had taken their seats, and Cort leaned over to ask, "When was I elevated to sainthood, and by whom?"

Liz shrugged, smoothing the napkin on her lap, regretting the impulse that had caused her to say what she had. But honesty won out, as it always did with her.

"Moira said the only men who would be able to put up with me were either saints or doormats. You're definitely not a doormat, so…"

Cort laughed softly. "Your cousin doesn't really know you that well, does she? If she saw how all the men in the hospital follow you longingly with their eyes wherever you go, she'd realize how silly she sounds."

Then he leaned in even closer so he was speaking right into her ear. "And my thoughts toward you right now aren't very saintly at all."

It made gooseflesh break out all up and down her arms.

And she knew Robbie wasn't the only Prudhomme who was going to be naughty between brunch and dinner.

CHAPTER SIXTEEN

IF THE BRUNCH was the epitome of elegance and refinement, the party that evening would best be compared to a rave. Giovanna had rented one of the hottest night clubs in Manhattan, complete with DJ, and invited a crowd of people who hadn't been at the actual wedding ceremony. Some of the older members of family and elderly friends forwent the evening festivities, but for those who attended there was a private upstairs lounge with a bar and comfortable chairs. There they could look down on the dance floor through the large windows or step out onto the balcony, which had a nice view of Central Park.

That was where Cort and Liz ended up, since neither of them were inclined to join the gyrating mass of bodies on the dance floor or have to scream to hear each other speak.

"Are you having a good time?" Liz asked Cort, as they stood on the balcony, sharing a drink and getting a breath of warm night air.

He smiled in response, casually looping his arm over her shoulder.

"You've asked me that at least a hundred times today. Yes, I've had a good time."

She couldn't help worrying. Her family could be heavy weather to those not used to them, her father's side filled with eccentrics sprinkled with snobs, her mother's with snobs sprinkled with eccentrics. And everyone knew the only difference between eccentricity and insanity was how much money the person had. No doubt Cort had been exposed to a lot more than just what she'd witnessed herself, since she'd been busy with wedding duties.

"Even with Aunt Bunny asking you if you were at the Battle of the Bulge? Or Francesca acting as though being a surgeon in a hospital, rather than in private practice, was akin to working as a pool boy?"

He laughed then, his arm tightening around her in a comforting hug.

"Your aunts were a delight, and it's not the first time my career path has been questioned, believe me."

Curious, she twisted slightly to look at him. "Really? How so?"

"Oh, my ex, the one who dumped me right before our wedding, seemed to think it would be more appropriate for me to be a plastic surgeon. I think she was hoping for free cosmetic work down the line."

Horrified, she actually gasped. "What? Did she understand the training you went through to be a trauma surgeon? The dedication it took to get to where you are, and how good you are at your job?" She huffed, disgusted. "How silly can people be?"

"I don't let it bother me. I've come a long way, and although I sometimes have to remind myself of that, the bottom line is life is good."

The door behind them opened and Robbie said, "There you are."

It was only when she turned, a smile already in place, that she realized her brother wasn't alone. Their parents stepped onto the balcony behind him and, on seeing Liz and Cort, seemed to hesitate for an instant.

Robbie grinned, one of his cheeky, inviting grins, and said, "I was hoping to get the chance to talk to you one on one, Dr. Smith. My father isn't the kind to ask what your intentions are toward Liz, but I don't have the same scruples."

"Robbie!"

Both Liz and her father said it at the same time, in the same warning tone, the similarity so marked they all just stood there for a beat.

And then Robbie said quietly, "Ah, nature wins out every time, doesn't it? You two are so alike, sometimes it's frightening."

Cort's arm had dropped away from her shoulders when they'd turned to greet the others, and Liz shivered, missing the comforting warmth. As though sensing her need for reassurance, Cort reached out and touched her wrist, his fingers rubbing back and forth a couple of times.

"I came prepared for an interrogation," Cort said, smiling. "And after spending time with your Aunt Millie, I'm confident I can stand up to anything."

"Ah, sir, I think you'll find she merely softened you up for me," Robbie replied with another grin and a sweep of his arm toward an unoccupied group of chairs at the end of the balcony. "After you."

With another light touch to Liz's wrist Cort strode off with Robbie, and she watched them go, trepidation keeping her gaze fixed on their retreating backs so she didn't have to look at her parents.

"Go with them, Brant," Lorelei said to her husband. "Make sure Robbie doesn't do anything to make Dr. Smith uncomfortable."

"Yes, darling," Brant replied, before bending to kiss her cheek.

Then he strode off, leaving Liz alone with her mother.

Lorelei smiled at Liz. "It all went well, don't you think?"

"Yes, Mom. It did."

Just moments before she'd thought this the perfect time to ask her mother about the past. Now she was kicking herself for her cowardice. Her mother's contented smile was well earned, and Liz was loath to see it disappear.

Then her mother said, "This is the first opportunity I've had to tell you how proud I was of you today."

Liz dredged up a little smile of her own. "It's amazing what a designer dress can do."

Lorelei's perfectly shaped brows rose. "Eliza, the woman makes the dress outstanding, not the other way around. I know I've told you that before."

"Yes, Mother," she said dutifully, having indeed heard it many times over the years.

Her mother huffed. "You're beautiful, Eliza. I think you're old enough now to know it for yourself and not dismiss me when I say it, the way you used to when you were a child."

The sharp retort was so surprising Liz only just stopped herself from gaping at her mother.

"What? When did I do that?"

"All the time. You'd quote that odious Nanny Hardy at me. 'Better to be useful than decorative.'" Lorelei made a sound as close to a rude one as Liz had ever heard from her. "And, of course, it's important to be a useful member of society. You becoming a doctor was the proudest moment of my life, because you worked so hard for it. But the way she went about it gave you a complex about your appearance, and that was unforgivable in my book. How I despised that woman."

"If you hated her so much, why did you keep her on?"

All the fire seemed to go out of Lorelei, and she turned to look out over the park. Although her back was ramrod straight, she seemed to droop.

Liz suppressed the sigh rising in her throat. "Mom, it's been a long day. Do you want to sit down?"

Lorelei shook her head. "I'm fine, Eliza. Why do all of you treat me as though I'm made of glass? I'm far stronger than any of you seem to think."

The echo of Cort's words gave Liz the courage she hadn't thought she'd ever be able to find. For so many months she'd avoided asking the questions she needed to ask to move through it, afraid of what she'd hear. Now she was ready, if her mother was willing.

"Mom, will you tell what happened all those years ago with you and Dad and Robbie? I really need to know."

Liz saw her mother's lips tighten, and then she nodded.

Turning so they were face to face, she said, "After you were born, I suffered from postpartum depression. Worse, I learned that, because of an infection, I would never have any more children. The only way I knew how to deal with it was to stay busy, take on more charity work, keep moving and be out all the time."

She lifted her chin, not defiantly but as though

taking ownership of something she hadn't been able to at the time.

"I was drinking too much, wouldn't even discuss what I was going through with your father, who tried to get me to go to therapy. It was as though I was outside myself, watching my life disintegrate around me, and could do nothing about it."

She fell silent for a moment, reached for Liz's hands. Gripping her mother's fingers, Liz waited, her heart heavy with sadness for all Lorelei had been through.

"We were young, Eliza, your father and I. I was barely nineteen when you were born, your father not even twenty-one. It's not really surprising we couldn't handle what was happening. I knew he was having an affair, even through the fog in my head, but I didn't care. I didn't care about anything."

"Oh, Mom."

"One night I came home, and I just couldn't do it anymore. I took a handful of sleeping pills with a glass of vodka and lay down, ready to get it all over with."

Without conscious thought, Liz stepped forward and hugged her, holding on as hard as she could, horrified by the knowledge she'd almost had to grow up without her mother.

Having her had never seemed that big a deal before, but now it did.

"Dad found me in time, and I was admitted to a treatment center." She pulled back, out of Liz's embrace, so she was once more looking into her daughter's eyes. "This is the important part, Eliza. We forgave each other, and made a promise to be honest, to stick together and never shut each other out again. Our love was strong enough to weather the storm of all that had happened. Made us strong enough to come out on the other side."

"But what about Robbie?"

"Brant broke off the relationship with his mother, and she left the firm without telling him she was pregnant." Lorelei shook her head. "I don't think she would have ever told Brant about Robbie if she hadn't got sick and been given a short time to live. I'll be honest, I was angry at first, but then I realized he was just a little baby who was about to lose his mother. I had enough love to give to both of you. How could I refuse to take him in? But..."

Something in her expression made Liz's stomach clench, brought a wave of defensiveness she couldn't seem to subdue.

"But what, Mom?"

Lorelei's eyes gleamed with tears. "But by then we'd realized you were the one affected most by what had happened."

"Me? How?"

"While we were running around, actively trying to ruin our marriage and life together, who was looking after *you*? For the first four years of your life we weren't there for you, weren't the loving, caring parents we should have been. *That's* why I kept Nanny Hardy as long as I did. I may not have liked her, but she was the one constant in your young life. How could I deprive you of that?"

Liz searched her mother's face, her eyes, unable to fully process what she was saying, her mind whirring with thoughts, memories, snippets of time she'd never consciously examined before.

Her first memories, not of her parents but of the nanny, the stern-faced woman who hadn't believed in hugs and kisses. Of being wary of the tall man she'd seen infrequently but had learned to call Daddy, and the beautiful stranger who had sometimes flitted into the nursery and then disappeared again.

All that had changed when Robbie had come, and she'd always thought it was because of him, his smiles and laughter, the love he so easily gave, that they had become a family. Now her mother was saying that wasn't the case, and Liz didn't know how to process this new information.

"All I wanted was for my children to love and admire me," her father said softly from behind them, having approached so quietly Liz hadn't known he was there.

She turned toward him, and her heart ached anew to see his face lined with worry. "I was afraid that once you heard the story you'd resent me, and that would break my heart. I… I hope you can forgive me, Eliza. I was so young, and so stupid. I didn't mean to cause any of you pain, and it's been the regret of my life to think I have."

"I hope you can forgive *us*," her mother added, laying a hand gently on Liz's arm.

"There's nothing to forgive, Dad, Mom," she said, her voice rough with the tears she was holding back. "I turned out okay, didn't I?"

It was a cry from the heart; a plea born of years of feeling disconnected, of thinking herself a disappointment to two of the people she loved most.

"Oh, baby." Her father pulled her into a hug so tight her ribs ached a bit. "You turned out perfectly. Far better than we ever deserved. And if we ever made you feel otherwise, it was probably because we were trying too hard to make up for what we'd done."

She didn't really understand what he was saying, too full of emotion to make sense of it all. But something broke free in her, releasing the kind of tenderness that cracked her hard shell of a persona only infrequently.

Leaning back in his arms, she reached up to smooth down his hair, and whispered, "Love you, Daddy."

And it was all worthwhile to see her father smile through the tears on his cheeks, as he pulled Lorelei into the circle of his arms too, for once the three of them in perfect accord.

At peace.

"'Being deeply loved by someone gives you strength, while loving someone deeply gives you courage,'" her mother murmured.

Liz leaned back, blinking away her own tears,

laughter rising in her throat as she said, "Mom! When did you start quoting Lao Tzu?"

Her mother sniffed delicately. "Please continue to underestimate me. I quite enjoy it."

"She's very special," Robbie said to Cort as they watched parents and daughter embrace. "And more than special to me."

Despite his warning, Liz's brother had made no effort to "interrogate" Cort. Instead, the conversation had been general, a kind of getting to know each other Cort wasn't sure was even necessary, since it was doubtful they'd meet again. As much as he'd enjoyed parts of the day, the one thing the experience had solidified in him was that he didn't belong, at all, in this world Liz so easily navigated.

It had felt surreal to see the way these people lived; like something out of a movie, where everyone was beautiful and money was no object.

And although he'd met some nice folks, he'd also been very aware of the pointed looks he'd received, and the snubs. There had even been a few comments, not directed at him but said in such a way he couldn't help hearing, wondering what Liz had been thinking, having him there.

Cort had wondered too, more than once, during the day.

"You don't have to worry," he told Robbie. "Liz and I really are just friends."

Leaning back in his chair, eyebrows raised, the other man gave him a considering look.

"I don't know you well enough to figure out whether you're a fool or you think I'm one."

Cort shook his head, looking once more over to where Liz and her parents stood, connected by bonds so strong they were almost visible, talking quietly together. The sight made him so happy nothing else mattered. Whatever they'd spoken about had obviously bridged the divide between them, and he knew how much it must mean to Liz.

"Your sister is an amazing woman, and I..."
Love her.

It wasn't a revelation. Not really. Cort was beginning to think he'd fallen for her from that first night in Mexico, and his feelings had grown with each subsequent encounter. But it was the first time he'd allowed himself to think it, to acknowledge it, because he'd known that doing so would just increase the inevitable heartbreak exponentially.

"You…?"

Startled out of his reverie, Cort said, "I'm sorry. What?"

Robbie replied, "You said Liz is an amazing woman and were about to add something about yourself before you stopped. I was curious to know what you planned to say next."

There was no way he'd share what he'd actually thought. He cleared his suddenly tight throat and replied, "I'm honored by her friendship. It means more to me than I can express, and I'll always treasure it."

"You should." The charming, smiling façade had fallen away from Robbie's face, revealing a shrewd, serious man. "She doesn't give her friendship easily, or lightly. When she loves, she loves with her whole heart, even if she doesn't express it the way most people expect."

The mention of love made Cort's heart clench with longing, and his gaze was drawn, magnetically, back to Liz.

How beautiful she was, with her face shining with joy as she looked at her father. She wasn't smiling, but that didn't matter. Anyone who knew her well would recognize her happiness, and Cort counted himself lucky to be in that number.

It was a sublime moment, but beneath his joy for her was his own inescapable aloneness. The knowledge he'd never known, and never would know, the kind of bond these people shared, one with the others.

Robbie sighed, a contented, happy sound. "I'm glad she's made up with Dad. In the end, family's all you have, you know?"

No, I don't.

But suddenly their affair made sense to him. Liz's distance from her father had left an emotional void in her life that perhaps, in some small way, her friendship with *him* had filled. Liz had needed something, a kind of intimacy, to distract from her anger and pain.

He'd done the same with Mimi, hadn't he? Using her as a crutch after Brody's death? Was he still doing the same with Liz? It felt different. He'd drifted into the relationship with Mimi, never feeling very strongly about her, or longing to see her when they'd been apart. On the other hand, Liz filled every corner of his mind, his heart, his soul.

For a moment, just a fleeting instant, Cort allowed himself to imagine what it would mean to be truly loved by Liz Prudhomme, not just as a friend and a sexual partner but as the one person made just for her. The thought overwhelmed him, elated him before he descended, with a crash of common sense, back to reality.

He took the last swallow of the Scotch in his glass, letting the fiery liquid slip down his throat, the burn reminding him that everything in life, no matter how delicious, had an attendant pain.

And nothing, especially anything good, lasted forever.

Now that Liz was reconciled with her family, it was only a matter of time before she realized how little he had to offer, and she left him.

Everyone else of importance in his life had done it. He didn't envision her being any different.

CHAPTER SEVENTEEN

CORT WAS TOTALLY unprepared for the effect that going to Liz's brother's wedding would have on his life. In his world a wedding was just a private event, and he'd had no idea Robbie and Giovanna's would also be a media circus, with repercussions that echoed into his work life.

At first he didn't know what was causing the shift in the way some of his co-workers acted around him, and tried to ignore it. Only after one of the nurses actually came out and asked him about it did it sink in that the entire hospital knew he'd gone to Robbie Prudhomme's wedding with Liz.

It turned out there were photographs and videos of the event all over the internet. Society websites had shots of the Prudhommes and their friends, while the mainstream media and gossip sites were more interested in Giovanna and her famous friends. To cap it off, some of the attendees had taken candid shots and uploaded those too. While Cort had stayed out of most of the pictures, there were enough of him and Liz together to get the hospital tongues wagging.

The worst of it came later in the week when he was cleaning up after an emergency small bowel resection.

Dr. Malachi, the anesthesiologist, who was washing up at the other sink, said, "You're a sly one, Smith. Going for the long money shot, huh?"

Surprised and confused, Cort looked at the older man, who was grinning over at him. "Excuse me?"

"Getting in good with the Prudhommes. It's a sound investment. After all, Hepplewhite was founded by one of their relatives, and it's their money that in part funded the hospital's renovations. If you hitch your wagon to that star, you're probably guaranteed a berth for life, like our ER specialist."

There was no mistaking the malice behind the statement, but it wasn't the implication aimed at him that made Cort contemplate exactly where he wanted to punch Malachi.

Aware of the surgical nurse, who'd stopped dead in her tracks, probably too surprised to pretend to be discreet, Cort reached for a towel to dry his hands, giving himself a moment to get his temper under control.

Then he stepped into the anesthesiologist's personal space, knowing he was looming over the shorter man in what could only be considered a menacing manner. But he kept his voice conversational, as though discussing the weather.

"Are you implying that Dr. Prudhomme is anything less than a stellar medical practitioner?"

Malachi blinked up at Cort, the grin fading from his face, to be replaced with a mingled look of fear and anger. "What? No—"

"Or that she wouldn't have every hospital in the city, hell, probably the country, clamoring for her to join their staff if she decided to leave Hepplewhite?"

Malachi took a step back but was stopped short by the wall behind him. His mouth moved but no sound came out.

"I know for a fact you're not suggesting that Dr. Prudhomme or her family felt it necessary to purchase her place on the staff here. Do you know how I know that, Dr. Malachi?"

"How?" the other man said in a weak voice,

when Cort raised his eyebrows and waited for a reply.

"Because I believe that would be slander, and I refuse to think that any member of staff at a hospital I work for would be capable of that."

Without waiting for a response, Cort turned and strode out of the room. Keeping his expression calm was a job in itself. Inside he was fuming and embarrassed.

Was that what people thought of him, that he was currying favor with Liz because of her family's wealth? Just telling himself those people didn't know him, so couldn't properly judge, didn't help. In reality it just fed into his own sense of unworthiness, solidifying the knowledge that he was, and would always be, an outsider, an interloper in Liz's world, and he believed she'd come to realize it too.

She had been distant since the wedding. Well, to be fair, she'd been extremely busy, back to working twelve-hour shifts and, on top of that, her parents had decided to stay in New York for a few extra days. Most of her free time was spent with them. He didn't expect that she'd want him hanging around with her parents, but Cort had hoped she'd find a little time for him. Yet, although she'd texted and they'd seen each other around the hospital, there'd been no mention of getting together.

Everything seemed to be pointing to the end of their relationship, as he'd suspected, and, as prepared as he'd tried to be for it, his heart had ached at the thought. Now, with the run-in with Malachi still fresh, and anger simmering beneath his skin, he almost looked forward to it.

It was time to end things with Liz, on his terms, before she got tired of him and told him to go. Abandoned him, the way everyone else in his life had.

At least this way he could salvage what was left of his pride, even though there was no hope for his heart.

Our love was strong enough to weather the storm of all that had happened. Made us strong enough to come out on the other side.

The words her mother had spoken at the wedding reception kept playing in Liz's head. They'd been revelatory for her. For a while, after their talk, she'd felt strange, as if the moorings tethering her to life had loosened or slipped, leaving her floating just above the ground. Everything had changed since Cort had come into her life, and she knew herself to be on the brink of a huge emotional shift. If she hadn't already gone over the precipice.

She'd needed time to sort it all out in her head, and hadn't really had the chance to do so properly, with the aftermath of the wedding and her parents' visit being extended.

Yet, in between working and time spent with her parents, she'd had a lot to ponder. Brant and Lorelei's story had explained so much, not just about why Brant had strayed but also about why she had felt somewhat disconnected from her parents. It truly was a moot point whether her character had come about through nature or nurture, but now she had no doubt it had been, at least in part, formed during those years in Nanny Hardy's care.

Knowing her parents were proud of her, even though they rarely expressed it, had also lifted a weight off her heart.

There was a sensation of being renewed, of being given a different perspective. She was still working through it but was looking forward to discussing it with Cort. In the past, she'd have called Jojo or one of her other close friends and talked to them. Now she felt as though only Cort would truly understand. After all, he was the one who'd given her the courage to speak to her mother.

Being deeply loved by someone gives you strength, while loving someone deeply gives you courage.

How true those words were, and taking the spirit of them into her heart she admitted, for the first time, that she loved Cort.

Not with the young, puppy-like devotion she'd lavished on Andrew, but with the deep, selfless, abiding love that lifted and elated, while never diminishing. Now she knew love didn't have to be a weakness but could be a river of strength.

This wasn't part of their deal, for her to fall for him, so she'd keep that to herself. It seemed unfair to burden him with her emotions. He'd made it clear that New York was just a waypoint.

Like her.

She'd texted him earlier and he'd said he'd come by, but he was late and now Liz found herself on edge. Caught up in her own ruminations and activities over the last week or so, it was only now that she realized he'd seemed a little distant.

Finally the doorbell went, and she went into the foyer to let him in.

It felt like forever since she'd seen him and, with her self-revelation fresh in her heart, she wanted to hug him, but something about his posture stopped her in her tracks.

"Hi," she said instead, hovering just inside the hallway, her heart suddenly pounding and her palms damp.

"Hello," he murmured in reply, locking the door and then turning to face her.

A cold lump developed in her stomach at his stern expression.

"Bad day?" She knew how it could be. A patient you thought you'd saved suddenly succumbing to their injuries, or one who you knew from the start was a long shot, but had hoped would recover simply couldn't be saved.

"You could say that," he replied, but didn't elaborate.

Normally she could tell what Cort was thinking, or at least gauge his mood, but today was different, and Liz wished she knew why.

"Want to talk about it?"

Why was she being so hesitant? Normally she'd

go in, guns blazing, demanding to know what had happened, but this time she didn't want to.

Cort shook his head. "Not really. And not right now. I have something else I need to talk to you about."

Silently, she led the way back into her living room and sat on the couch. Instinctively, she knew whatever it was he was about to say wouldn't be good. Bracing herself, she allowed all the changes that had come over her in the last week and a half to fade, being replaced by the cold, stoic persona she'd carefully cultivated over the years.

Crossing her legs, she looked up at him as he paced a few feet into the room and stopped. Keeping her expression noncommittal came surprisingly easily, old habits reasserting themselves without effort.

"What is it?" she asked, pleased by how cool she sounded.

"I heard from an old army buddy that they're looking for trauma surgeons, and I'm planning to reenlist."

There was no reaction inside her, except for a thickening of the ice already building in her chest.

"Hawaii?" she asked, in a mildly curious voice.

His eyebrows rose slightly, as though surprised she remembered what he'd said all those months ago.

"No, Germany."

"Well, that'll be interesting too." How distant she sounded, as if she didn't care, while inside she was dying. "Maybe the elusive Hawaii transfer will follow."

For a moment his stern façade seemed to crack, and she glimpsed something dark, painful behind his gaze. It touched something deep in her soul, melted the ice around her heart.

This was, after all, Cort. The man who'd broken her hard shell into so many pieces she doubted she would ever truly be able to put it back together, no matter how she tried. The man who'd given her the courage to face up to her fears, comforted her when her demons had torn her apart, given her the type of uncomplicated, passionate friendship she'd secretly dreamed of but had never believed she'd find.

Taken her battered, closed heart, both soothed it and opened it wide. Reawakened her to love.

He'd never lied to her either. She'd known this day would come, and had to let him go without revealing the tears building behind her eyes, the burning pain in her heart.

For once in her life her restraint was appropriate. He didn't deserve to see her pain.

With a deep breath, she said, "Cort, I'm going to miss you. What we've shared has been so special, so real and true, at least to me. I knew this day would come, and if this is what you want, I'm happy for you. I hope you find joy on your travels."

Dark fire gleamed in his eyes for an instant and then died, and he said, "Liz, I wish I could stay longer, but I can't."

She held up her hand, stopping him. "I'm not asking you to. I made myself a promise never to expect anyone to give up their dreams for me. I know how that feels, how it can sap your determination, your courage and ambition. I... I just needed you to know how I feel."

Cort nodded, seemed set to say something more but, instead, turned and walked away.

The closing of a door had never sounded more final.

She cried then, wishing she could have told him how she truly felt. Wishing it wouldn't have made him feel badly to know she loved him and wanted him to stay.

Forever.

CHAPTER EIGHTEEN

HE SHOULD BE RELIEVED, glad that Liz had taken it so well.

Instead, his insides were in constant turmoil, and he couldn't get more than a couple of hours' sleep a night, bedeviled by memories, pain, sadness.

It was the right thing to do. He'd told her from the beginning he wouldn't be around for long, that he'd learned not to get attached to anyone. He wasn't even sure what he felt for her was love. How did you recognize something you'd never experienced? Never known?

No, he'd learned his lesson long ago.

Nothing worthwhile lasted.

Better to move on before she did, or before he couldn't.

Seeing Liz around the hospital was agony. He'd been expecting her to give him the cold shoulder, but she simply acted the same way she had all along, with cool professionalism and no drama whatsoever. The rest of the staff watched them, since the rumor mill had them pegged as a couple, and he got the impression many of them were disappointed when there were no overt displays of affection. If only they knew how many places in the hospital Liz and he had snuck to and made love!

But that was something he tried very hard not to think about. Bad enough when he turned a corner and was sideswiped by a memory of Liz, hands upraised, gasping as he held her on the edge of passion.

They'd laughed about the day they'd almost got caught in the old isolation ward, once it was far enough in the past for him to find it amusing. Liz teasing him about how angry he'd been.

If anything, it was her companionship, the shared laughter he missed the most. Liz had become such an important part of his life he was lost without her in it.

It would get better once he was out of New York City, back in the military milieu. The army had suited him. The discipline. The order. Life would go back to normal after he reenlisted.

He'd already received the paperwork from the army medical corps command. They were sitting on his desk, ready to be signed, and he'd been contacted to ask when he would be available to report for duty. He'd explained he'd need to give ample notice to Hepplewhite and had been informed the army would do whatever was necessary to assist him getting out of his current contract asap.

He'd put off signing the paperwork for weeks, although he'd made up his mind to do it. It was, he told himself, because he dreaded facing Gregory Hammond. The older man had recently been singing Cort's praises and broadly hinting that, in a couple of years when he retired as head of surgery, he hoped Cort would take his place.

His army friend who'd told him of the need for trauma surgeons had called the night before and told Cort, in rather inelegant terms, he had to make up his mind immediately.

"Time waits for no man, Cort. And the army waits even less."

Now, seeing Liz in the hallway, leaning on the nurses' station desk as she checked a chart, cemented his determination.

It was the way his heart painfully contracted and his stomach clenched that did it. The time to move on was past. If he didn't get it done now, he might be stuck mooning over her for another five months, until his contract expired.

He didn't think he could stand it.

Getting an appointment to see the chief of surgery the next day should have been a relief. Yet he spent the entire night staring at the window of his bedroom, absolutely sure Liz's scent was still on his sheets, despite them being freshly washed.

The following morning he went in early and stood for a moment outside the hospital, looking up at the building. No matter how much he told himself he wouldn't miss it, or the city, he knew it was a lie. It had grown on him, giving him a sense of home he'd never had before.

"Hey."

And that was why.

He turned to see Liz walking toward him, the car that had dropped her off driving away.

"Hi," he replied, not trusting his voice to say anything more.

"I'm glad I saw you," she said, her cherries jubilee voice wrapping around him, enticing and arousing. Yet there was a hint of hesitancy in her voice as she continued, "I have something for you."

"Oh?"

For a moment she looked unsure, and then her chin came up and she gave him one of her straight-on, clear-eyed looks.

"Yes," she said, in her decisive way. "I... You mean a lot to me, Cort, and knowing you're leaving, I wanted to do something for you. Something you probably wouldn't do for yourself."

Mean a lot to me. The words would have made him laugh if the pain in his heart wasn't so severe. It sounded so tepid in comparison to how he felt. Standing there, her fresh, sweet scent washing over him, he just wanted to lose himself in her eyes, in her arms, her body.

He blinked, glanced away in an effort to get himself under control.

"You didn't have to do anything for me, Liz. You've done more than you can ever know."

She had taught him to love. Given him joy, and hope, and this terrible agony, knowing she would never love him back.

"I wanted to anyway."

There was something different in her voice, a dark emotion roughening the already deep tones.

He looked at her in time to see her take a deep breath and push her shoulders back, as though bracing for his reaction.

"I know you said you weren't interested, and it made no difference to you, but I was talking to Robbie, and he said that knowing where he had come from had made a huge difference in his life. So I hired a private detective, and I think she's found your parents."

For a moment all the air left his body. Light-headed, he stared at her, wondering if he'd heard her correctly.

"It's not as bad as you thought, Cort. If these are your parents, and all the indications are that they are, they didn't abandon you. You were kidnapped."

There was a low wall behind him and he eased down onto it, unsure whether his legs would continue to hold him up.

"Liz…why…?"

She tilted her head, her eyebrows scrunching together in a frown.

"You deserve to know, Cort." She hesitated for a moment and then her lips firmed. "You told me you'd learned not to get attached, and I know how badly it hurt you to lose your friend, but everyone needs to have people on their side. People—family—they can turn to in times of need, or sorrow, or happiness. I... I wanted you to have that, if it was possible, even if it isn't with me."

Still numb, he took the outstretched envelope from her hand and lifted the flap. The report was several pages thick, but it started with a summary. It took him a moment to be able to focus, to make sense of the words, and gather the threads of the story.

Child Sean Gallagher, went missing from the home of his parents, Kevin and Florence Gallagher. Signs of break-in. Father's ex-wife, known drug and alcohol abuser, was also missing from the small town in Wyoming, and suspected of taking the child. The ex-wife was eventually found, deceased, in Seattle, Washington. While the child was not found with her, some articles of clothing and a stuffed animal known to have belonged to Sean were found with her body. Attempts to trace where the woman had been in the two months prior proved fruitless.

"How can your PI be sure these are my parents? What makes her sure?"

He didn't want to acknowledge the hope gathering in his chest. *Nothing good lasts forever. Don't place your hope in people, because they always let you down, hurt you. Leave you.* These were the mantras he'd taught himself, that life had taught him, and he didn't want the pain of finding out this was wrong. That this family wasn't his.

"The timing is right," Liz said gently. "And Kevin Gallagher came to the States from Ireland, while Florence is from the Shoshone tribe. The DNA matches too."

It was too much. Too unexpected. Too promise-filled.

Could it really be that once he'd had a home, been a part of a family that had wanted him, loved him, perhaps, thinking he was gone forever, mourned him? It all but broke him, thinking of it, as longing he hadn't known still existed inside his soul washed through him, like a storm.

No. That was a lie. He'd known the longing was still there. He'd felt it every time he looked at Liz, held her in his arms, experienced the passion flowing between them. That longing was what had frightened him so much, made him determined not to give in to the love.

Then her words came back to him, making his heart stumble over itself again.

She'd said she wanted him to have a family, *even if it wasn't with her.*

The fear of rejection should have made him keep his mouth shut, but hope and want and need overwhelmed him and he had to ask, "Did…did you really want to be my family, Liz?"

"I did," she said, almost defiantly, holding his gaze, even as hers filled with pain. "I never meant to love you. I knew you would leave, and I should have guarded my heart better, but—"

He didn't let her finish, just pulled her into his arms. "I'm glad you didn't. Tell me it's not too late, that the home I've found in you is still mine."

Liz didn't hesitate.

They'd wasted too much time already.

Hardly able to believe what was happening, she held him as tightly as she could.

"Of course it is. Forever," she whispered into his ear.

"I love you," he said, burying his face in her neck, neither of them caring about the other staff members coming and going nearby.

This was too important to worry about propriety and hospital gossip.

"Tell me you love me again."

"I love you, Cort. I always will. Even if you have to go."

He shook his head. "How can I give up the best thing that's ever happened to me? I haven't signed the papers, and now that I know you love me too, I won't."

She pulled back, so she could see his eyes, and replied, "If you really want to reenlist, and you wanted me to, I'd go with you. Being with you is more important than anything else."

She needed him to know she was serious. He knew how much she loved New York, and Hepplewhite, and hoped he recognized she would give it all up for him if he wanted her to.

Cort swept a finger over her cheek.

"I don't want to reenlist, love. That was my fear making me run. Even though I've never known what love is, I knew I'd fallen for you, and was afraid of the heartache."

Tears stung her eyes as she shook her head. "You might think you didn't know what love is, Cort, but everything you do, the way you deal with people, your compassion and strength, tells me you have so much of it to give."

"It's all for you," he said, turning his hand to capture her fingers.

"Perfect," she replied. Then she took a deep breath, knowing there was one last thing they had to get out into the open. "What's been happening around the hospital…"

"You mean the speculative looks I've been getting because of your brother's wedding?"

She cringed, having heard about his encounter with Dr. Malachi. She knew he'd been subjected to sideways looks and not-so-subtle questions from some of the staff who'd seen the pictures online.

"Yes. Please don't let it bother you. People's reactions have been completely ridiculous."

He gave her a lopsided grin. "It hasn't been easy, having people question my motives regarding our relationship. But I'll get over it. You're too important to lose over something so stupid."

Liz sighed. "I'm sorry Robbie's wedding was the introduction you got to my family. It really wasn't a proper first meeting. They're all a lot more normal than that circus implied."

"You have to admit it was over the top, to put it mildly. It was like being in a movie."

"It was, but the only reason was because Robbie married Giovanna, and she's a supermodel. If he'd married Jane Brown from down the road, no one would have cared, and there certainly wouldn't be pictures all over the internet."

He leaned back slightly to look at her, his skepticism obvious, and she shrugged. "We can always avoid my family functions from now on. Or just run away somewhere where no one knows us. How about Mexico?"

Shaking his head, Cort tightened his grip. "Oh, no. I've found my version of paradise right here, and I'm not leaving. Although we could go back to the scene of the crime for a visit, to see if the honeymoon suite still lives up to its billing."

"Can we leave now?" she asked, ravenous for him, inwardly cursing having to go to work in a few minutes. "I want a chance to make sure you're convinced I'm the woman for you."

"I don't need convincing." He leaned in, so their lips were just a breath apart, teasing them both. "I'm yours, now and forever, and I'm not letting you go."

EPILOGUE

Two years later

IT WOULD HAVE been nice for it to be a quiet night for once.

Liz snorted at the thought as she strode out of one ER cubicle and headed straight for another, stripping off her blood-splattered gloves and gown as she went. Unfortunately, there had been an incident at a street carnival a couple of blocks away from the hospital, and so far they'd had a couple of stabbing victims, a gunshot victim and three people who'd been hit by a car all come in at the same time.

That was on top of the usual volume of emergency cases.

"Trauma team's on its way, Dr. Prudhomme," a nurse called out, as Liz slipped past a couple of police officers standing guard just outside the gunshot victim's cubicle.

"Thirty-two-year-old male, Sylvester Mc-

Kenzie, gunshot wounds to the upper thorax and upper left thigh," the paramedic told her, as she started her examination, then listed the vitals and observations they'd made on the way to the hospital.

"Sylvester, my name is Dr. Prudhomme. I'm going to be looking after you. Can you tell me where it hurts?"

The reply was a profanity-laden rant from behind the oxygen mask, aimed at the police, the paramedics, and Liz herself.

"Hey, enough of that."

How was it that after all this time her heart still leapt whenever Cort entered the room?

Sylvester added Cort to his list of rant-worthy topics, but when Liz glanced at him, Cort just gave her a little wink before turning back to the patient.

Before long Sylvester didn't have enough breath left to rant about anything. His blood pressure started to fall too, and X-rays showed one bullet lodged in his lung. Yet it was the leg wound that worried Cort even more. Sylvester had been shot while driving his car, the bullets going through the door before striking him, and

Cort suspected the lower one's trajectory might have caused serious injury.

"Here," the radiologist said, pointing to the screen. "The bullet has done damage to the femur and pelvis."

"I was afraid of that," Cort said. "We're going to have to get him stabilized enough to get him up to Angiography. I need to see what veins and arteries have been damaged before I go in there."

Liz's heart sank. Pelvic injuries were notoriously tricky.

As they headed back to Sylvester's cubicle, Cort muttered, "Can we move up our reservations if I get stuck in the OR?"

It was the anniversary of the night they'd met in Mexico, and they'd decided to celebrate. After all, they'd agreed it had been one of the best nights of their lives, and the luckiest.

"If that happens, I'll call and ask them to prepare something for takeout."

Cort looked at her and shook his head. "Only you could call one of the hottest restaurants in town and ask for takeout."

Liz gave him a wink. "I sweet-talk all the chefs

and staff, so that if such an occasion arises, I'm golden."

Then Cort the lover was gone, and Dr. Smith was back; focused, cool as ice.

"Let's get him stabilized, stat. I need to know how much damage was done by that bullet and get in there to repair it as soon as possible, or we'll lose him."

After they got Sylvester stabilized, Cort headed off with him to Radiology and then from there to the OR.

When Liz finished her shift, she went up to the surgical floor to see whether they were having a nice dinner out tonight or staying in.

One of the nurses at the station said, "I think they're just finishing up, Dr. Prudhomme. Dr. Smith should be out soon."

"Thank you." She waved, going to one of the lounge areas and sitting down to wait. If they didn't leave in an hour, it would be takeout for sure. Once Cort came out of surgery, he'd let her know whether he could leave or not.

Liz stretched, suppressing a yawn. She actually wouldn't mind takeout tonight, rather than having to go home and dress up. They'd had a busy couple of weeks, with Cort's parents coming for a visit from Wyoming and his sister Misty flying in from Chicago too to celebrate Flo's birthday in New York with Cort. Unfortunately his brother Connor couldn't join them this time, since his wife was expecting their second child and, although her due date was still a few weeks away, she hadn't been given the all clear by her ob-gyn. The nice thing was that Connor and his wife lived just down the road, so to speak, in Philadelphia. Cort and Liz had already visited them a number of times, and planned to go back as soon as the baby was born.

It had been a busy time, but also a pleasure to have the Gallaghers come to stay. They were wonderful people; warm, caring, and so incredibly happy to have their son back.

They'd never given up on him, even after all those years, and the hardest part for them was getting used to calling him "Cort" rather than "Sean."

"I'm too old to get used to a new name," Cort had said. "Plus all my degrees are in this one. It would be a huge hassle to change them, even if it were possible."

She'd heard a hint of regret in his voice, but conceded the point.

The back of Liz's neck tingled, and she twisted in the chair to see Cort coming down the corridor toward her, still wearing his surgical cap, although he'd removed the gown. It was funny how she always knew when he was around, as though an invisible string stretched between them and vibrated whenever they were close to one another.

Rising and picking up her bag, she went to meet him in the hallway.

"Takeout tonight?" she asked, even though she suspected she already knew the answer.

"Maybe just cancel altogether. He's in pretty bad shape, and I have a suspicion I'll be here quite a while longer. Chez Ramone's food isn't that great heated up at home."

She was used to it, of course she was. They both had days when plans had to be changed or abandoned, but it didn't stop her feeling a little disappointed. From the sound of it, he wouldn't be home before she had to go to bed, since she was working an early shift in the morning.

"Well, in that case, let me give you your gift now," she said.

Cort gave her a lopsided smile. "You bought me a gift?"

"Mmm-hmm," she replied, digging the brochure out of her bag and handing it to him.

He read it, a huge grin breaking across his face.

"Greece?"

"Yes. Cruising from island to island. I want to make sure we keep scratching those itchy feet of yours so you never get tempted to run away. Oh, and next year, when Connor's baby is old enough to travel, I think we should plan a trip with both families to Ireland."

Cort shook his head then bent to give her a chaste, if slightly lingering kiss, and it was enough to heat her blood, make her want to go in for a deeper, harder one.

"There's no chance of me taking off anywhere without you, babe. I'm home to stay, right here in your arms."

"Glad to hear it," she said matter-of-factly, but she knew he could read her better than anyone, and he saw the love in her eyes. "That's the way it should be."

* * * * *

LET'S TALK
Romance

For exclusive extracts, competitions
and special offers, find us online:

f facebook.com/millsandboon

⊙ @millsandboonuk

🐦 @millsandboon

Or get in touch on 0844 844 1351*

For all the latest titles coming soon,
visit millsandboon.co.uk/nextmonth